The Play of Daniel:
Critical Essays

Edited by Dunbar H. Ogden

With a Transcription of the Music
by A. Marcel J. Zijlstra

EARLY DRAMA, ART, AND MUSIC
Monograph Series, 24

MEDIEVAL INSTITUTE PUBLICATIONS

WESTERN MICHIGAN UNIVERSITY

Kalamazoo, Michigan
1996

ISBN: 1–879288–76–1 (Casebound)
ISBN: 1–879288–77–x (Paperback)

Library of Congress Cataloging-in-Publication Data

The play of Daniel: critical essays / edited by Dunbar H. Ogden ;
    with a transcription of the music by A. Marcel J. Zijlstra.
        p.   cm. — (Early drama, art, and music monograph series ; 24)
        Includes bibliographical references and index.
    Contents: The staging of the Play of Daniel in the twelfth century
/ Dunbar H. Ogden — Divine judgment and local ideology in the
Beauvais Ludus Danielis / Richard K. Emmerson — The play of Daniel
in modern performance / Fletcher Collins, Jr. — Music in the
Beauvais Ludus Danielis / Audrey Ekdahl Davidson — The play of
Daniel (Ludus Danielis) / transcribed by A. Marcel J. Zijlstra.
    ISBN 1–879288–76–1 (casebound : alk. paper). — ISBN 1–879288–77–x
(pbk. : alk. paper)
        1. Liturgical drama—History and criticism. Danielis Ludus.
I. Ogden, Dunbar H. II. Zijlstra, A. Marcel J. III. Danielis
ludus. IV. Series.
ML178.P65 1996
782..2'98–dc2O   96–27276
                                                      CIP
                                                      MN

Contents

Introduction 1
    Dunbar H. Ogden

The Staging of *The Play of Daniel* in the Twelfth Century 11
    Dunbar H. Ogden

Divine Judgment and Local Ideology
in the Beauvais *Ludus Danielis* 33
    Richard K. Emmerson

The Play of Daniel in Modern Performance 63
    Fletcher Collins, Jr.

Music in the Beauvais *Ludus Danielis* 77
    Audrey Ekdahl Davidson

The Play of Daniel (*Ludus Danielis*) 87
    Transcribed by A. Marcel J. Zijlstra

Translation 117

Index 127

ILLUSTRATIONS

Egerton MS. 2615, fols. 95–108 . . . . *Plates* 1–27

Introduction

Dunbar H. Ogden

Often performers seek to reconstruct a piece of music as it was originally produced, but that cannot be done with a drama. Here lies the dilemma in staging *The Play of Daniel (Ludus Danielis)*. In singing the chant there are relatively narrower interpretive margins. We may conjecture that at Beauvais the *Daniel* was sung *a cappella* by the Schola. The pitches of the notes are known, as is the church where it was performed. But the original rhythms of the music are more problematic. Yet for a modern ear we can come close to re-creating the sound of twelfth-century *Daniel*.

The opposite holds true for the drama. In searching for ways to deliver its original spirit as drama, we discover that the interpretive margins are immense. Words change over time and convey different emotions, thus telling a quite different story. How, then, can the *Daniel*—with its twelfth-century characters, customs, and means of dramatic expression—be best staged for a twentieth-century audience? For the musical element in the *Daniel* the director must make choices within a fairly narrow range concerning such matters as rhythmic values; whereas for the dramatic impact one must choose within an enormous range, beginning with facial expression, gesture and body language, movement and movement patterns, costume, props, set pieces if any, and lighting. Were those lions left to the imagination of the twelfth-century audience, or did they actually show themselves in Beauvais Cathedral? Should they appear in performance today? It is inevitable that such questions must be in the minds of the contributors to this book, which has as its purpose the goal of understanding the *Daniel* and of considering its interpretation for modern audiences.

For the *Daniel* this means penetrating and elucidating its twelfth-century contexts and then searching for equivalent twentieth-century contexts. "From a modern point of view," wrote French

1

stage director Michel Saint-Denis, "certain periods in the past are closer to us than others. For instance, the English popular tradition as exemplified by Shakespeare is closer, I believe, to a man today, even to a Frenchman, than French aristocratic art of the seventeenth century as exemplified by the plays of Racine."[1] It occurs to me that the recent burst of medieval plays and music in our churches, theaters, and concert halls reveals new perceptions of affinity between our own times and the Middle Ages: a longing for the simple purity of the chant, for the possibility of belief, and a search for identity in a fragmented, uncertain, confusing, violent, technocratic, and materialistic world.

The character of *Daniel* focuses on faith, the faithfulness of one person in particular—a person whom the original performers characterized as young like themselves. The very first lines of the play emphasize that it was the young people (*juventus*) of Beauvais, presumably of the Schola associated with the cathedral, who devised it. Designed for a feast of inversion dominated by the subdeacons and the youth of the cathedral,[2] the play gave the students of the song-school the opportunity of empathizing with Daniel as a young person. They even brought him closer to them geographically by having him sing a few lines in French, in the local dialect, instead of the play's Latin. They could admire his resistance against misdirected authority and the prophet's ability to decipher what was hidden to rulers and wise men. They could also identify with his taking of risks and, snatched from the very jaws of death, his final vindication and triumph. Further, his God was their God of Beauvais. His faith gave him the wisdom to interpret dreams and visions. What was mysterious to others became clear to him. His God, in turn, protected him and delivered him from bondage and death. Therein lies the emotional center of the drama. Each contributor to the present collection approaches that dramatic center from a particular point of view. Each brings a specialty and skill both in scholarship and in practical performance experience.

In my study I seek to record what is known about the ecclesiastical space for which the *Daniel* was originally composed, and I analyze its stage directions with this space in mind. Richard K. Emmerson examines the cultural dynamics of the twelfth century: the *Daniel* as containment of traditionally boisterous festivities and also as manifestation of the civic and ecclesiastical power of Beauvais. Fletcher Collins, Jr., surveys modern performances and indicates the actual production choices made by people who have staged the *Daniel* in our times. Audrey Ekdahl Davidson gives attention to musical characteristics, especially the singular mixture of ecclesiastical and secular music that marks the *Daniel*. She suggests musical impact on an audience as familiar with popular troubadour-trouvère melodies as with chant melodies.

"It is obvious that to give life to the works of the past cannot mean 'reconstruction'," wrote Michel Saint-Denis. "Reconstruction of the past is dead. Neither can we imitate the past. It has to be re-created from a contemporary attitude." Performance of the *Daniel* constitutes an act of re-creation, not re-construction. Furthermore, the performance of a play depends, first of all, upon the original scenic disposition with which the play is connected naturally and umbilically—that is, to the local milieu and period where and when it was written. Saint-Denis underscored with italics his conviction about the "*close relationship between the visible shape of the stage and the form of the written play.*"[3] Nowhere does that hold true more strikingly than for the music-drama of the medieval church.

Of all theaters in the world, the Romanesque and the Gothic church of the Middle Ages holds in and of itself the most power. Perhaps only the ancient Greek theater can be said to have matched the medieval church's awesome stone presence, its mystery of light and incense, its air of celebration, its echo of the human community at prayer and song, its compass of the quotidian and its reach toward the divine—and its invitation to performance. The medieval church still endures, both in actual structures and in modern replicas. We can still play the liturgical drama there, where the liturgical drama was born.

In a sense one might say that the present volume was conceived in a church, albeit a modern structure in which the medieval design was modified in ways that nevertheless provided a splendid performance space. This church was the Cathedral of Christ the King, Kalamazoo, Michigan, surrounded by six hundred medievalists. There the *Daniel* was performed by the ten-member Schola Cantorum "Quem Quaeritis" from the Netherlands as a centerpiece of the annual International Congress on Medieval Studies in 1994.

During the previous winter, A. Marcel J. Zijlstra, Music Director of the Schola, had made a fresh transcription of the play directly from the original manuscript, Egerton MS. 2615, in the British Library. Meanwhile I had studied the rubrics and compared them with similar rubrics in other liturgical dramas. The object was to start with the most accurate words and music possible: thus the facsimile and the new transcription published here.[4]

It is a truism that a musical composition, a drama, or a dance is not complete in its manuscript or printed form, whether it consists of notes, or words, or choreographic notation. Each requires the evanescent moment of performance. The human voice, for instance, can create shadings at which musical notation can only hint, and sometimes in the most unsuspected ways human voices can shape coherence from what may seem disjointed in a score. At the farther range, there is no such thing as one definitive performance of the music, the drama, or the dance. The very nature of a performing art lies in its ever-changing surfaces. If the musician, the actor, or the dancer delivers an inner truth of the composition to the audience on a given day, then the performance is right.

While the dramatic text of the *Daniel* is a score for actor-singers, its performance is an act of interpretation. To carry it out with integrity we thus need to have two elements. We must have a score that accurately reflects the original, in this case Egerton MS. 2615, which, to be sure, includes a thirteenth-century copy of *Daniel* from an earlier manuscript. And we need to understand as well as possible the original aesthetics that inform the play—that is, its twelfth-century cultural contexts, performance conditions, and audience reception.

Regarding the congregation of audience-worshippers, for instance, the rubrics do not indicate that in medieval church performances they joined with the chorus in singing the final canticle, the *Te Deum laudamus* (*We Praise Thee, O God*), but they often did sing a hymn in the vernacular.[5] The text of the *Daniel* specifies closing with the *Te Deum*, while no rubric mentions congregational singing. Quite obviously those of the cathedral community who knew the *Te Deum* would have joined in the singing, while members of the laity who did not would have remained silent. What should twentieth-century practice be in regard to such practice? Would inviting our audiences to join with the performers in chanting the final *Te Deum* serve to translate the core of the *Daniel* experience? Or would such participation mistranslate? Where it would have been wholly natural for a medieval congregation, would it be unnatural for a modern audience? Would being called upon to imitate a medieval practice even go so far as to block the aesthetic or spiritual experience of a modern audience?

In the Cathedral of Christ the King we did in fact invite the members of the audience to join with the Schola in singing the closing *Te Deum* because they were all medievalists, some of whom sang the *Te Deum* weekly, some daily. On this occasion they sang with gusto, many of them by heart. However, with any other except a highly specialized gathering we might not invite such participation. In other contexts such singing along might be uncomfortable, disruptive, awkward. We wanted to sing more than just the notes; we wanted to sing the song. From this underlying wish we came to a rule of thumb: in contemporary drama performance, never do something merely because it was done in the Middle Ages; in contemporary music performance, always do something because it was done in the Middle Ages—at least as a point of departure.

In further examination of medieval and modern attitudes, the role of Daniel provides a revealing case study. As a dramatic character, for instance, he embodies a double vision of the Jews, two juxtaposed views of the Jewish community: one dominant, the other subdominant. Daniel is the hero of the play, Daniel is a Jew, and Daniel is a prophet who foretold the birth of Christ—another hero, explicitly Jewish. The conflicting view of the Jews manifests itself when at the conclusion Daniel prophesies the end of the "kingdom of the Jews." Nowadays it is necessary to take great care in coming to grips with attitudes toward Jews in various times and places during the Middle Ages. "A real translation is transparent," wrote literary critic Walter Benjamin. "It does not cover the original, does not block its light." For Benjamin the context leads the translator beyond the words on the page: "In all language and linguistic creations there remains in addition to what can be conveyed something that cannot be communicated; depending on the context in which it appears, it is something that symbolizes or something symbolized."[6] At the writing of the *Daniel* the Jews had not yet been expelled from

France. In that regard the *Daniel* presents a two-fold sensibility. Daniel and his fellow captives are sympathetic people in the drama, Daniel a man of great courage and wisdom. Daniel is referred to specifically as Jewish. Eventually he will foretell that Christ will be born in Bethlehem of Judea.

Initially the Babylonians are the enemy, the oppressors. Their imperialistic Babylon is doubly juxtaposed with victimized Jerusalem: politically, as oppressor vs. oppressed; and morally, as seat of wickedness vs. seat of holiness. The despicable act that brought the downfall of both Nebuchadnezzar and Belshazzar (Balthasar in the play, following the name given in the Vulgate) was the destruction of the "temple of the Jews"—and the Babylonians' looting of sacred temple vessels for their own debauchery. There can be little doubt that the vessels from the sacristy of Beauvais Cathedral were used in the play as the sacred vessels from the temple of the Jews. At the play's finale, freed by his God from the lions' den and fed by the prophet Habakkuk, Daniel foretells the Nativity and the end of the Jewish kingdom: their "anointings also will be no more." However, there is not a hint of ethnic anti-Semitism. Quite the opposite. The implication of Daniel's message is religious: non-believers in the Nativity will not be part of the City of God. But, and herein lies the seeming contradiction, Daniel the Jew is true to his belief in his God, who is actually the Christian God of Beauvais.

For the performers of these roles the space of a Beauvais Cathedral yields vital understanding of the *Daniel*. As I explain in my article in the present book, the *Daniel* was composed for a Romanesque church in Beauvais, built prior to the present thirteenth-century cathedral but known to have provided ample space for the eight or more processions specified by the manuscript. This space must have been acoustically very resonant with a height of more than sixty feet. Thus the ideal space in which the work might be unfolded today in performance will need to provide aisles and galleries along which the singers might process and sing. And the space needs to be employed both as a musical and a theatrical instrument. Speaking from my own experience, during rehearsal the performers grow sensitive to the cathedral as visual and aural instrument. Through listening in that space and breathing its air and walking along its aisles and galleries and feeling its dimensions, through allowing the space to penetrate them, they are better able to absorb the *Daniel*—and better able to re-create the inner experience of the work. As singer-actors they acquire greater authority and integrity.

Emmerson demonstrates in his study that the *Daniel* became "a textualized counterpart of the cathedral" which reflected the "local traditions of Beauvais." He views the play in performance as a manifestation of the city's complex relations with the French crown. In that sense the performance not only displays political and social self-understanding but actually creates it. Emmerson concludes: "the *Ludus Danielis* represents in dramatic form the proud local traditions of Beauvais in contrast to the national claims of Paris and its increasingly powerful monarchy." Thus if a contemporary seeks the inner life of the *Daniel*, he must first seek out the *Daniel*-and-Beauvais history.

Collins reveals how various modern music and theater directors have gone about this process of translating from the musical score to the stage. Beginning with Noah Greenberg in 1958, many have constructed scenes and machines, laid a great amount of electrical cable, and added arrays of medieval musical instruments. But, as Collins points out, overall one can perceive a sort of spectrum, with opulent pageantry at one extreme and a spare monks-in-the-cathedral style at the other. The present volume does not attempt to establish any specific production style as the ideal but only to insist on integrity in performance, whether actual or imagined.

Most important, perhaps, for the twelfth century and for our time is the performance of the music. It is because of the music that the *Daniel* lives on today in our churches and concert halls. Davidson, in her essay, shows the *Daniel* to be a remarkable aggregate in which musical elements are joined together to produce a masterful work of dramatic art. She teaches us, for instance, to hear the pattern in which musical "repetitions build up suspense for the elucidation of the riddle which appears in the last three appearances of the melody." She also poses for us the musical problem of irony. For example, in regard to the setting of the *Gaudeamus*, she writes, "The jubilant text, steady rhythm, and words of praise and rejoicing are, in the light of Balthasar's fate, ironic." And she concludes by calling our attention to the overarching shape of the music, to the way in which "the music both accompanies and carries the action in the drama from moment to moment, from unrest to climactic tension to this finale in rest and revelation" as the Angel sings the Nativity hymn *Nuntium vobis fero de supernis* (*I bring you a message from high heaven*).

Zijlstra's transcription of the *Daniel* together with the facsimile of the manuscript are intended to provide the reader with primary materials for study and eventual production. A transcription is, of course, necessarily an interpretation. Usefully, the transcription published here has been tempered in the experience of live performance. Just as one must make choices in translating from one language to another, so one makes choices in translating from a medieval manuscript to a modern score. In this particular case, as Zijlstra explains in his note to his transcription, it is a written record of what worked best for the singers and the music director while playing and singing the *Daniel* in the Netherlands and in the United States. The solutions, then, are not purely academic but are tutored by professional practice. The transcription is intended for anyone interested in how the play *can* (not *should*) be performed musically. At the same time, one can compare it with the original, the facsimile. A reader with theoretical musical knowledge may well be astonished by the choice of meters. Were other possibilities adopted in the twelfth century? We do not know. But in performance these proved to be the best ways of solving the musical problems.

Without the work of Clifford Davidson as producer, editor, and friend, the production of the *Daniel* by the Schola Cantorum would never have been staged in Michigan, and this book would not have come into being. The British Library kindly gave permission for the reproduction of the facsimile of the play from Egerton MS. 2615. And finally I wish to thank Travis D. Williams for bibliographic assistance as well as F. A. Rowe and Roger Travis for their help with matters of translation.

NOTES

[1] Michel Saint-Denis, *Theatre: The Rediscovery of Style* (1960; rpt. New York: Theatre Arts Books, 1976), p. 50.

[2] See the seminal article by Margot Fassler, "The Feast of Fools and *Danielis Ludus*:

Popular Tradition in a Medieval Cathedral Play," in *Plainsong in the Age of Polyphony*, ed. Thomas Forrest Kelly (Cambridge: Cambridge Univ. Press, 1992), pp. 65–99.

Rubrics also specify the character of Daniel as a youth (*aetate juvenus*) in the twelfth-century Anglo-Norman *Ordo Repraesentationis Adae*, in the thirteenth- and fourteenth-century examples of the *Ordo Prophetarum* from Laon (*adolescens*) and Rouen (*juvenilem vultum habens*); see *Medieval Drama*, ed. David Bevington (Boston: Houghton Mifflin, 1975), p. 117; Karl Young, *The Drama of the Medieval Church* (Oxford: Clarendon Press, 1933), II, 145, 158.

[3] Saint-Denis, *Theatre*, p. 57.

[4] For my description of the performances of the *Daniel* by the Schola Cantorum "Quem Quaeritis" at the Cathedral of Christ the King and subsequently at the Church of the Transfiguration (Little Church Around the Corner) in New York City, see "Census of Medieval Drama Productions," ed. Peter Greenfield, *Research Opportunities in Renaissance Drama*, 35 (1996), 147–52. For the New York production, see also the review by Melody S. Owens in *The Early Drama, Art, and Music Review*, 17 (1994), 56–59.

[5] For example, I count texts of the *Visitatio Sepulchri* from over thirty different localities where the rubrics explicitly indicate that the people were to sing the German hymn *Christ ist erstanden* either before or immediately after the *Te Deum*; see Young, *The Drama of the Medieval Church*, Vol. I, and Walther Lipphardt, *Lateinische Osterfeiern und Osterspiel*, 9 vols. (Berlin: Walter de Gruyter, 1975–90), *passim*.

[6] Walter Benjamin, "The Task of the Translator," in *Illuminations*, ed. Hannah Arendt (New York: Schocken, 1969), p. 79.

The Staging of *The Play of Daniel* in the Twelfth Century

Dunbar H. Ogden

While the *Ludus Danielis* contained in British Library, Egerton MS. 2615, has frequently received scholarly attention, little effort has been made to illuminate its original theatrical context.[1] It is the purpose of the present essay to examine the available evidence, such as it is, concerning the probable conditions of production at Beauvais Cathedral in the twelfth century. The initial areas of inquiry must involve the architecture of the cathedral, the liturgical calendar, and the scholastic community at Beauvais. Thereafter I will focus in some detail on the rubrics of the *Daniel*.

I

In 1975, *The Play of Daniel* was performed at Beauvais by the Clerkes of Oxenford,[2] but of necessity the extant thirteenth-century Gothic cathedral replaced the original twelfth-century staging place of the *Daniel*. Thus, while the 1975 production might seem to have been a performance closest to medieval production conditions, it fell short in at least one important respect—its architectural setting—and, therefore, in its *mise en scène*. *The Play of Daniel,* usually dated to c.1140 although it may be twenty or thirty years later and is preserved in a unique manuscript that is later yet (1227–34),[3] would have premiered in the Romanesque cathedral known as the *Basse-Œuvre* which preceded the present cathedral as the main place of worship in Beauvais. After a series of fires in the late twelfth and early thirteenth centuries,[4] the *Basse-Œuvre* was systematically demolished to make way for the much larger present cathedral. Today only the western end of the nave of the *Basse-Œuvre* remains standing next to the present Beauvais Cathedral.[5]

11

Unfortunately, therefore, the architectural setting at Beauvais must ultimately remain a mystery because most of the *Basse-Œuvre* no longer exists. Nevertheless, some very plausible assumptions concerning the earliest performances of *The Play of Daniel* can be made based on the experience of modern productions of liturgical drama and on archaeological findings. With regard to the usefulness of modern performances, Andrew Hughes writes: "When directing actual performances, I am extremely conscious that scholarship is *never* complete until the result has been seen in practice: on the boards, necessity always reveals something about the texts or chants that could never be imagined in the abstraction of a study."[6] This statement applies as well to spatial concerns as to musical matters. With regard to *The Play of Daniel*, the usefulness of actual production for understanding the play was recognized as early as the first modern performance by the New York Pro Musica under the direction of Noah Greenberg at The Cloisters in 1958. Quite correctly E. Martin Browne noted: "Remembering that the play was created at the period when the magnificent series of cathedrals and great churches which enrich the European scene were just built or in building, we realize that the authors of such plays as *Daniel* were skillfully exploiting the opportunity offered by the great architectural spaces for pageantry and display."[7]

In Greenberg's edition of the play Nikos Psacharopoulos also pointed to a fact that has become quite obvious on account of experimentation in the production of the drama: "The play was originally conceived, of course, for performance in a cathedral or church, and the ideal setting for a contemporary production—with the various exits and entrances for the players, the aisles for processions, and the chancel as the staging area for the drama—is still the church."[8] Psacharopoulos is joined by Jerome Taylor and David Wulstan in positing the apse and choir of the cathedral as the place of action (although the nave probably also served as staging area, as discussed below).[9] But what can really be said about the apse and choir? Or, for that matter, what was really there for the young men of Beauvais who were the composers of the *Daniel* to exploit in the *Basse-Œuvre* as they put the play together?

The *Basse-Œuvre* was apparently a grand cathedral for its architectural style and period. Architectural historian Émile Chami writes that recent archaeological research has revealed here "a development similar to the great Carolingian cathedrals."[10] Furthermore, bits of wall paintings, colored glass, and ceramics "attestent l'abondante ornementation de l'extrêmité orientale de la Basse-Œuvre," and "son abondante ornementation, peinte ou sculptée, était d'une richesse comparable à celle des grandes églises de l'époque."[11]

Since the transept would be in close proximity to the apse and choir, the grand dimension and intricate detail of the *Basse-Œuvre* as documented in these citations would indicate a large and dramatic space for the *Daniel*. Indeed, Taylor, in his consideration of the Balthasar scenes as profaned liturgical services, develops a number of parallels between sacred objects of the church and the props of the play:

> The fully dramatic action begins precisely when, not a priest, not the bishop, but the personified Balthasar is enthroned in the *cathedra*, where he does not belong. . . . Balthasar sings for the sacred vessels, which will be brought from sacristy to altar not for the eucharistic banquet but for feigned profanation.[12]

No banquet table is specified, and hence one wonders, by extending Taylor's premise, if the actual high altar was conscripted for use as the table for Balthasar's feast of debauchery—a scene in which he parodies a bishop. What is most important here, then, is the probable use of the *cathedra*, or episcopal throne, in the play itself. The rubrics of the play specifically mention a throne, and the use of the *cathedra* for this purpose would strongly situate the performance of the *Daniel* in the cathedral itself, if this point were ever in doubt. It would, of course, be interesting to know if there was an altar of Holy Daniel that might have served as the focal point of Daniel's house.[13]

The height of the *Basse-Œuvre* may also be significant. Chami reports that "the nave was nine meters wide and rose to nearly nineteen meters."[14] Two aisles flanking the nave, one to the north and the other to the south, made the total width about twenty meters. The roof height of these side aisles is not known. If the chancel-apse area was as high as nineteen meters, the dramatic possibilities for the writing scene of the *Daniel* are obvious since this significant moment could be raised well above the rest of the action. Certainly the present Cathedral of Beauvais dwarfs the remains of the *Basse-Œuvre*, but at a width of twenty meters and a nave height of nineteen meters the older building would have been no small structure for the tenth and eleventh centuries—a point borne out in aerial photographs.[15]

The most important architectural consideration for the *Daniel*, however, is the east choir in its relation to the church in its entirety, especially when seen as an extension of the nave. The archaeological evidence is clear: the *Basse-Œuvre* was a long church for its time. With 52.5 meters of its length still remaining, Chami writes, "one can assume that the length of the entire cathedral originally surpassed sixty-five meters."[16] Indeed, the great length of the *Basse-Œuvre* may have been necessary to accommodate a large congregation, which eventually grew to such a size as to require a new cathedral altogether. As Stephen Murray notes, the choir in particular "was of considerable length, since it would have to provide seating for a sizable chapter,"[17] but more space was apparently needed also for the laity.[18] The entire east end of the building was apparently elaborately decorated. As Chami reports, in 1974 numerous fragments were collected "which can be compared in their workmanship to the very beautiful face of a man discovered in 1971 from a tenth- or early eleventh-century fresco that decorated the early choir of the *Basse-Œuvre*."[19]

It is no accident that such expressive human faces emerge in the visual arts precisely at a time and a place where role-players acted out a range of human emotions in the drama. In regard to staging space, Beauvais' long and well-decorated choir would have been put to good use in the *Daniel*. As Browne noted concerning the first modern performance by the New York Pro Musica, "Within a playing-time of barely an hour we have a dozen processions, some of them accompanied by great pomp."[20] Such a large number of processions is unusual[21] and points to the availability of architectural space as well as the liturgical occasion, which also very likely invited such effects. In any case, the benefits of a long choir will be immediately obvious as soon as the actual production of the play is contemplated. In the processionals of Balthasar, the Satraps, and the Queen, the long choir would allow for extended display of pomp and finery passing through the choir and along the nave, and back again. Alternatively, the length could work to the opposite effect in

Daniel's procession since thus the extended introduction of the lone, isolated figure, "pauper et exulans" ("a poor man and an exile"), would be intensified. Even more possibilities exist. During the invasion of Darius, the choir-nave length would heighten and prolong the tension inherent in a major reversal of the play, while the comic aspects of Habakkuk's scene (if indeed it contains comedy) would be assisted by the additional time required to traverse a long choir and perhaps part of the nave as well. In any case, the possibility of a long choir put to multivalent uses throughout the play must only have added to the architectural contribution provided by the apparent grandeur of the *Basse-Œuvre*.

II

While the story of Daniel belongs to the Old Testament, specific attention is given in *The Play of Daniel* to the birth of Christ, and this clearly locates it in the liturgical calendar as a drama firmly linked to the Christmas festivities. For example, the conductus for Daniel on fols. 103ᵛ–104ʳ proclaims:

> Congaudentes celebremus natalis sollempnia;
> Iam de morte nos redemit Dei sapientia.
>
>   . . .
>
> In hoc natalitio
> Daniel cum gaudio
> te laudat hec contio. (ll. 270–71, 276–78)
>
> (Let us together joyfully celebrate the solemn feast of the Nativity;
> God's wisdom has now redeemed us from death.
>
>   . . .
>
> On this feast of the Nativity,
> Daniel, this crowd honors you with joy.)

And at the end of the play, Daniel utters a prophecy derived from liturgical usage:

> Ecce venit sanctus ille sanctorum sanctissimus,
> Quem Rex iste iubet coli potens et fortissimus. (ll. 385–86)
>
> (See, that Holy One comes, the holiest of holies,
> Whom this strong and powerful
> King orders to be worshipped.)

Finally, the Angel suddenly appears and sings the final words of the drama:

> Nuntium vobis fero de supernis
> natus est Christus dominator orbis, in Bethleem Iude,
> sic enim propheta dixerat ante. (ll. 389–91)

> (I bring you a message from the high heaven:
> Christ is born, Ruler of the world,
> In Bethlehem in Judea, as the prophet foretold.)

W. L. Smoldon's account of the various Christmas observances provides a useful starting point concerning the position of the *Daniel* within the liturgical calendar:

> The medieval festivities of the Christmas Season included a number of special celebrations, ruled in turn by four different ranks—the deacons on St. Stephen's Day (Dec. 26th); the priests on the Feast of St. John (Dec. 27th); the choristers on Innocents' Day (Dec. 28th, when the licensed humours of the Boy Bishop took place); and finally the despised subdeacons, who presided on three other days, including the Feast of the Circumcision. The activities of the subdeacons, most notorious in France, received a variety of names, none of them complimentary, e.g. *festum follorum, stultorum* or *fatuorum,* which phrases can be summed up in the term 'Feast of Fools.'[22]

The *Daniel* seems most closely associated with the choristers and subdeacons. The connection to the first of these is verified by the play's text, which indicates that boys were in fact involved in the production as performers; however, less may ultimately be made of the statement at the beginning of the play that identifies the composers as the "youth" of Beauvais and addresses the audience with a statement of their intent. While involvement of young people is demonstrated, the younger boy choristers are not necessarily the youths who composed the music and wrote the text of the drama.

The connections of the *Daniel* to the subdeacons are also very strong and point to traditions identified with 1 January, the day in the Christmas octave that was associated with their participation in a feast given over to foolery and activities often criticized by reformers.[23] In the Egerton manuscript, the *Daniel* is preceded by an *Officium Circumcisionis,* and Wulstan plausibly saw this as evidence that they were both performed on the same day, 1 January—a point that has been accepted by Margot Fassler, who has offered new evidence to support the connection of the play with the festivities of this day.[24] Young, who had tentatively placed the drama on the previous day, had recognized the appropriateness of an arrangement in which it would be brought "into close association with the feast of Fools, and from the famous Prose of the Ass attached to those revels an echo has been discerned in the exclamation *O hez*, uttered by Darius."[25] However, on account of the careful work of Fassler, we can now be quite certain about the placement of the *Daniel* within the liturgical calendar—that is, not on the eve of the Feast of the Circumcision but on the very day. The play, in her view, resulted from the concerted effort by the Bishop of Beauvais to put down the more inappropriate and boisterous activities of the subdeacons. As such the play was related to the attempt to reform the Circumcision Office as presented in the Egerton manuscript. The play thus was also in Fassler's view designed to provide opportunities for *play* at the same time that it would preserve a decorousness that had not previously been present in the festivities of this day.[26]

The placement of the *Daniel* in the liturgical day was almost surely during Matins since the final direction of the text is for the *Te Deum* to be sung.

III

The Play of Daniel begins with a direct address of its originators to the audience-congregation about themselves and their play:

> Ad honorem tui Christe,
> Danielis ludus iste,
> In Belvaco est inventus,
> Et invenit hunc iuventus. (ll. 1–4)

> (In your honor, Christ,
> This play of Daniel
> Was devised in Beauvais,
> And it was the youth who made it.)

Who were these young men, and what do we know about the cathedral school with which we presumably need to associate them? Karl Young remarked that "Illuminating information concerning the cathedral school of Beauvais for the twelfth and thirteenth centuries seems not to be available,"[27] yet enough evidence now exists to piece together a partial but plausible representation of the physical environment in which the *Daniel* was probably composed.

The archaeological evidence seems to reveal several structures around the *Basse-Œuvre* that could have supported a scholastic community. In the early 1970's the remains of a religious building were discovered near the *Basse-Œuvre* that make "the existence of a post-Carolingian episcopal complex in Beauvais quite likely."[28] More such discoveries followed, and hence "one can reasonably suggest that they correspond to the annexes which were constructed at the same time as the church: the sacristy, the scriptorium, the archival hall or library, etc."[29]

In addition to the physical evidence, there is of course the intellectual milieu in which the school participated. As part of this milieu, a dramatic lineage may be posited for the *Daniel* in the work of the scholar named Hilarius who had written a Daniel play that probably preceded the Beauvais *Daniel*. The Beauvais *Daniel* indeed has a number of similarities which it shares with Hilarius' play.[30] Hilarius, who seems to have been a wandering scholar, and Ralph of Beauvais apparently were both students of Abelard; the latter went on to teach at Beauvais in the twelfth century.[31] While it may be speculated that Hilarius visited Beauvais at some time, it is safer to suggest that Ralph or another scholar brought his work to the cathedral school's library, where its connection to the Christmas season made it a likely model for the Beauvais composers. The general belief is that the Beauvais *Daniel* borrowed from and improved upon Hilarius' play. Indeed, recalling the term *invenit* from the Beauvais introduction, Wulstan remarks quite correctly that "*Invenio* means 'to find', implying the act of compilation, arrangement and refinement."[32] Hilarius' play is usually considered less refined than the Beauvais *Daniel*, and Young sees this as a factor in the lineage of the two plays, for "It seems unlikely that if Hilarius had the Beauvais version before him, he and his collaborators would have so generally renounced its superior dramatic and literary qualities."[33] In creating a play with the object of reforming the festivities of the Feast of the Circumcision, the Beauvais authors thus would have had before them a model upon which they could draw. Their play, however, is a wonderfully fresh creation and not a slavish copy. As Young notes, "In literary detail the play of the Beauvais students differs from that of Hilarius most noticeably in the dignity and gusto of the choral pieces, and in the presence of a certain number of sentences and phrases in French."[34] Unfortunately, we are not able to compare the musical structure of the two plays, since Hilarius' play has not come down to us with music. We therefore do not know if the Beauvais composers had a musical model. In any case, they were able to arrive at a play which has been rightly praised by C. Clifford Flanigan as "a liturgical cursus of incredible splendour—and of great literary and musical ingenuity."[35] And Susan Rankin has high admiration for the play and its "melodic invention, matching each different poetic form (of which there are many) with a new group of melodic ideas."[36]

Certainly the *Daniel* reaches for its inspiration beyond the Latinate religious world to the more secular culture, with which Hilarius too would presumably have had much contact. The significant existence of secular elements in the *Daniel* has not been lost on commentators. "Dare I say," says Smoldon, "that *Daniel* is one of the leading treasure-houses of medieval secular music?"[37] Other evidence also indicates that Beauvais was a sophisticated center of musical creativity.[38]

A final indication of the richness of the community at Beauvais does not involve the school directly except insofar as it was itself enriched by the work of artisans, particularly those who lived in the local region. This richness is, of course, confirmed by archaeological findings that point to fine workmanship at Beauvais before, during, and after the heyday of the *Basse-Œuvre*—workmanship that indeed must have contributed to that cathedral's splendor, which has been noted above. Chami observes: "In the substructure of the church . . . painted ceramic potsherds have been collected from the post-Merovingian era, prior to the eleventh century, that were virtually unknown in France until very recently."[39] Elsewhere he describes discoveries belonging to the tenth-century transept: a frieze of acanthus leaves and a head with a nimbus "of very fine workmanship."[40] Further, "[t]he craftsmanship of the faces and the techniques employed seem to indicate that these paintings are the work of an atelier belonging to the same school as the one which decorated the choir of the *Basse-Œuvre* and which has left us a precious example of its art in the wonderful face of a man discovered in 1972 inside Saint-Pierre Cathedral."[41] Thus the artisans of Beauvais were quite progressive in either bringing new methods from other locations to Beauvais or inventing these methods themselves. And just as their faces and bodies seem to take on new life, so also the drama at Beauvais seems to come alive. In any case, the archaeological information only adds to the total picture of Beauvais as a cosmopolitan center of musical and artistic creativity—a picture which makes perfect sense when we consider that this city produced that great example of dramatic art, the *Ludus Danielis.*

IV

While, as demonstrated above, much can be known in a very general way about the physical setting of the Beauvais *Daniel*, there is an important route to knowledge about more specific aspects of the original staging, and this is through examination of the rubrics. The rubrics reveal two remarkable characteristics of the *Daniel*: the sweeping use of ecclesiastical space and the liveliness of the acting, the latter being particularly appropriate for the Feast of the Circumcision. Such stage directions allow one to work out a few minimal spatial arrangements, while comparison with the rubrics of other liturgical dramas will throw further light on the play. At the same time, this kind of comparative study is capable of yielding a deeper understanding of the terms in the *Daniel* rubrics for vocal expression, gesture, and mimetic action. A staging of the play in our own era must begin with precisely these rubrical and textual clues as glossed by analogues from other examples of the liturgical drama.

In comparison with the extant corpus of the liturgical drama, the stage directions in the *Daniel* call for an enormous amount of action, of coming and going. To begin with, at least eight and possibly more processionals punctuate the performance—for example, the entry of the Satraps bearing the sacred vessels, and the pomp of the Queen's arrival. Two of the processions are marked *prosa* in the manuscript; five are marked *conductus.* These are useful musical designations. However, the rubrics say nothing in any definite way about the use of space *per se* in the *Basse-Œuvre.* Stage directions in a multitude of other liturgical dramas name specific altars, a tomb, or a portal where the performers pause to sing a piece of music or play out a particular action. The rubrics of the *Daniel* are silent on these matters. They do not mention the high altar or an altar of Holy Daniel. They refer neither to the choir nor to the nave, neither to a crypt nor to a westwork. But if other similar liturgical dramas are any indication, the performers of Beauvais must have employed the nave, aisles, crossing, and west end as well as the great east choir—the whole extent of the interior space. One can assume therefore that for a medieval audience the sound of *Daniel* came from everywhere. So did the movement.

What then is the firm evidence? It is possible to be absolutely certain in the case of the specified processionals and of references to localities. There is the previously mentioned throne (*solium*) for the King; eventually Daniel will sit next to him. Recourse to parallels in other liturgical plays of the period is very much in order here. Herod has such a throne in the twelfth-century Christmas play from Montpellier,[42] and several thrones appear in the slightly later Tegernsee *Antichrist*.[43] In fact, a space may have been marked off in Beauvais as the King's palace, for at one point the Satraps are described as "leaving the palace" (*relicto palatio*). Perhaps it was a platform. But where it was positioned, we do not know—possibly, like other set pieces of this sort, at the entrance to the east choir or in the crossing. Daniel has a house (*domus*), at some remove from the throne. A *domus* is called for in four of the twelfth-century plays from the *Fleury Playbook*.[44] And there is the lion pit (*lacus*). In the thirteenth-century *Joseph* from Laon there is also a pit—*lacus*, also referred to there as *cisterna*, *puteus*—where Joseph is secreted.[45] The lion pit in the *Daniel* is located at a level lower than the throne because King Darius "descends" to it. It had to have been large enough for Daniel to enter it. The rubrics and the lines do not indicate whether the audience actually saw Daniel with the Angel and the lions inside the pit. Daniel is led to the pit, the King goes over to it, and Habakkuk is led to it—all movements suggesting distance. Therefore it would seem that in the *Daniel* the following localities are distributed through the entire church: the throne (with a nearby seat for Daniel) and indication of the palace; the lion pit; Daniel's house; the entry and exit point of the Queen; and Habakkuk's place

("*Angelus reducet Abacuc in locum suum*" ["The Angel takes Habakkuk back (from the pit) to his (original) place"]).

Some possibilities concerning localized space immediately appear
evident. King Balthasar (and later Darius) could have occupied the
Bishop's throne, and Daniel could have descended into the crypt as
the lions' den. From the very inception of the liturgical drama, in
the tenth-century *Visitatio Sepulchri* at Verdun, the crypt was used
as a staging place.[46] Rubrics for the twelfth-century *Visitatio Sepulchri* at Sion and the thirteenth-century examples at Trier and Würzburg explicitly name the crypt beneath the east choir as the Holy
Sepulcher where the exchange between the Angel(s) and the Marys
actually takes place.[47] Thus the entry to the crypt, visible to those in
the church above, becomes an important position in the *mise en
scène*. Characters stop and sing there when about to descend into
the crypt or when reentering from it. A side chapel, ideally with an
altar dedicated to Holy Daniel, may have served as Daniel's *domus*
where the audience-congregation must have seen him in prayer.
With such an arrangement, no additionally constructed scenery
would have been needed, and indeed the addition of cheaply-made
scenic devices would have been in harsh contrast to the sophisticated and elegant setting which was the cathedral itself.

A possible analogue to the palace and the house could be the
castellum of Emmaus in the *Peregrinus* play.[48] Apparently this was
simply a platform or otherwise built-up structure in the crossing (*in
medio navis*) of Rouen Cathedral in the thirteenth century; similar
solutions appeared in the thirteenth-century Benediktbeuern (*Carmina Burana*) manuscript and in a play at Padua where Jesus and
the two disciples take a meal together after the Resurrection. In the
particularly relevant twelfth-century *Peregrinus* from Beauvais, the
two disciples lead Jesus to what is called there a "lodging" (*ad hospi-
tium*). Then, dramatizing the biblical narrative, Jesus breaks bread
with them and suddenly vanishes. Thereupon the disciples get up
and, according to the rubrics, search for him throughout the church
(*vadant per ecclesiam quasi querentes eum*) before returning *ad
Chorum*.[49] As in the *Daniel*, so here too the expanse of the architectural interior becomes the staging space.

It is surely dangerous if not downright wrong to superimpose
modern sensibilities on the Middle Ages. However, twentieth-cen-

tury experience in staging this drama in extant medieval churches
reveals just how convenient existing raised spaces and chapels are
for *mise en scène*, just how powerful is the invitation to move
through those spaces and to sing in them, just how extensively the
processional liturgy employed the great stone-wood-glass-and-cloth
instrument of the medieval architectonic structure in its entirety,
just how compelling the symbiotic relationship was between ongoing
processes of liturgical practice and ongoing processes of architectural
building, just how tuned the voices of the singing and the places of
the singing were (and are) to each other—and just how jarring most
forms of constructed scenery are in their contrast with the solidity
and beauty of permanent ecclesiastical structure and ornamentation.
In the same vein, contemporary experience with staging the liturgical drama in its original ambience also begins to reveal the
subtlety of light-play—sunlight and candlelight—that accompanied,
enfolded, and highlighted the liturgy through the day from dawn to
dark. So, for instance, at the finale of the *Daniel* one must begin to
imagine the physical light that suffuses the Angel who sings the
Christmas-birth announcement.[50]

Fassler has pointed out another dimension in her observation
that Darius absorbs elements of the horseplay of the usual high-
spirited antics of the subdeacons when he "becomes a veritable Lord
of the Asses, at the very moment in the play when he is duped by
jealous counsellors seeking to destroy Daniel"—a point at which the
Prose of the Ass, Orientis partibus, is the source of his melody.[51]
Such parody would, of course, have added energy to the depiction of
this pagan king, whose behavior would be seen as returning to
decorousness at the release of Daniel from the den of lions.

Mimetic action, gesture, and emotional expression with the voice
make for a theatrically vivid performance. Often the rubrics in the
liturgical drama yield no clues as to body language and vocal color-
ing. But, to the contrary, the rubrics of the *Daniel* call expressly and
in detail for graphic and vigorous acting. The words of the stage
directions themselves convey the animation, for they require ascend-
ing and descending, entering, leading, bringing in and carrying out,
hastening, running ahead of others, applauding, kneeling, worshipping, pointing at, looking, hearing, bearing and taking food, and
even pulling a prophet along by the hair. Several demand violent ac-

tion, some related to the political homicide—expelling a victim and killing him—while others are related to the lion pit—seizing a person, casting or throwing him into the pit, threatening with a sword, stripping of clothing, and devouring by lions.

Together with these calls for action, the rubrics also indicate a fine sense of timing, a modulation of scenic rhythm. For example, a processional, and arrival ensues, and then a burst of action, and an aftermath. One feels an overarching pattern where the blocks of action are carefully shaped, forming individual moments and moving from one transition to the next. As the story unfolds, so a concomitant urgency heats the dramatic atmosphere. The physical pace picks up. There is hastening. With the approach of Darius and his court, two of his soldier-courtiers run ahead of him, expel Balthasar from the throne, and appear to kill him as King Darius then "is seated in majesty." The timing of that scene must be exactly right. Or, to choose another example of pacing, at the finish of the play two Angels must act quite suddenly. When Daniel is tossed into the lion pit, instantly (*statimque*) an Angel threatens the lions with a sword, while, at the very end of the play so as to create a rhythmic climax, the Angel of the finale appears suddenly (*ex improviso*) to sing the glad tidings of the Christmas season.

Correspondingly the rubrics also call for vivid vocal expression: Balthasar is stunned (*stupefactus*) by the mysterious Hand; he cries out (*clamare*); other characters exclaim (*exclamare*) and exclaim joyfully (*gaudens*); they give counsel clandestinely (*secreto dicent*), give orders (*iubere*), pass on commands (*precipere*), and admonish (*admonere*). At one point the King speaks "not knowing" why a question has been put to him, and later he must answer "against his will" (*velit nolit*).

In the corpus of the liturgical drama comprising some 1,200 examples the following terminology is, I believe, unique to the *Daniel* rubrics: *applaudere* (to applaud), *exclamare* (to exclaim), *relicto palatio* (leaving the palace), *expellere* (to expel), *quasi interficientes* (seeming to kill [in Hilarius' version of the *Daniel*: *quasi interficiens Baltasar*[52]]), *precipere* (passing on a command), *rapere* (to seize), *comminuere* (to weaken, to threaten), *apprehendere* (to seize), *cum expoliati fuerint* (stripped of their clothing), *consumere* (to devour). The list in itself reveals the unusual forcefulness of the action and the sense of theatricality inherent in the play.

But most of the terms in the rubrics of the *Daniel* are also found in other liturgical dramas, and these may assist in understanding what a given stage direction in the *Daniel* is specifying. As previously noted, Balthasar in the *Daniel* is *stupefactus* (stunned) at the sight of the mysterious Hand. So is the Virgin Mary at the Angel's news of her pregnancy in the Christmas Play of the thirteenth-century Benediktbeuern manuscript; and so are the disciples at Emmaus when Jesus in the thirteenth-century Rouen *Peregrinus* suddenly vanishes from their midst.[53] A parallel to the regicide (*quasi interficientes*) is found in the non-liturgical Anglo-Norman play of *Adam*, designed to be performed outside the doors of a church. There at Cain's murder of Abel the rubric reads: "And he [Abel] will have a pot hidden in his garments, which Cain will strike violently, as though killing Abel [*quasi ipsum Abel occideret*]."[54] In these instances the word *quasi* underscores the sense of make-believe and draws a boundary where the author wishes to define theater by articulating the difference between an act and the imitation of an act.[55]

The use of food on stage does not occur in the *Visitatio Sepulchri* or in the Magi and Shepherd plays of Christmas. But in the remainder of the canon many major moments are set at a banquet or involve eating. For instance, the breaking of bread in the context of a meal takes place in the *Peregrinus* play, where Jesus divides a loaf of bread and says a blessing, and then all at once he disappears. In the twelfth-century Fleury *Peregrinus*, a table holds an uncut loaf, three wafers, and a cup of wine; there is first a washing of hands, and then after the ritual blessing Christ goes away explicitly while the two disciples are eating.[56] Meals are also served in the Fleury plays of *Lazarus* and *The Son of Getron* as well as in the Benediktbeuern Shorter Passion Play;[57] food is prepared in the twelfth-century Vorau *Isaac*.[58] So too does food create the center of a scene in the Beauvais *Daniel*: a meal (*prandium*) is carried and offered; the food (*cibum*) is accepted by Daniel. These are mimed actions.

Genuflecting occurs frequently and in various forms in the liturgical drama. In the *Daniel*, two characters bend their knees (*duo flexis genibus*). In like manner, Christmas Magi and Shepherds genuflect at the manger; and at times Mary Magdalen and the three

Marys genuflect before the Risen Christ. The act of homage is also described with the verb *adorare*. Daniel is seen worshipping his God (*adorare*). The same word is used in the Fleury *Herodes* to describe veneration at the Christmas manger by the Shepherds, the Magi, and the bystanders in the congregation.[59] We know, however, that the gesture of prayer with hands joined so commonly seen in late medieval art would not have been characteristic in such a scene, since it was a thirteenth-century innovation, allegedly imported from Buddhist practice.[60]

The act of running characterizes the versions of the *Visitatio Sepulchri* containing Peter and John. The text always says that they run to the Tomb, while a rubric often reinforces the movement. At Rheinau the younger man, John, explicitly runs ahead of Peter, the older man (*iuniore seniorem precurrente*), in a thirteenth-century *Visitatio*.[61] In the *Daniel*, the killers of Balthasar run ahead of an approaching procession to do the job.

Yet another common gesture involves indicating or pointing to an object or person. In a later scene in the *Daniel*, the Satraps show the law to Darius (*ostendent ei legem*). What are they doing? What props are they using? One finds a similar moment in the *Herodes* of Fleury where, according to the stage direction, Scribes actually bring out books, turn through the pages, and, showing the birth-of-Christ prophecy to Herod, explicitly "point with the finger" (*osten<den>tes cum digito*).[62] The gesture also occurs in the *Visitatio Sepulchri*, often in the versions containing the encounter between Mary Magdalene and the Risen Christ. Upon her return from that meeting at the Sepulcher, the Disciples ask her, "Dic nobis, Maria?" ("What have you seen, Mary?"), and she shows or points to the Tomb, and, if present, to the Angel(s), sometimes even to the grave-cloth. The texts from the nunneries of Barking and Origny-Sainte-Benoîte, both of the fourteenth century, as well as several other French texts indicate specifically that she should point "with her finger."[63] The evidence of the visual arts would call for a slightly crooked index finger since a fully extended finger would be a sign of accusation.

In regard to the emotional delivery of lines in the *Daniel*, Darius descends from his throne, comes over to the pit, and calls out to Daniel tearfully (*lacrimabiliter*). In the *Visitatio Sepulchri* of c.1400 at the Cathedral of Coutances, the Marys, approaching the Sepul-

cher, sing tearfully (*dicant voce lacrimabili*) the words "Quis revol-
vet" ("Who will roll away the stone?").[64] More frequent in the liturgical drama is singing joyfully (*gaudens*) and, even more frequent,
crying out (*clamare*). Darius exclaims joyfully at the rescue of
Daniel. Christmas Magi and Shepherds celebrate *gaudens*, for example, at Fleury, while also at Fleury the Innocents open the *Ordo
Rachelis* with a procession *gaudentes* all along the nave of the
church.[65] So too do the Marys at the close of the *Visitatio Sepulchri*
when they announce the Resurrection, as in the case of the Chorus
at Dublin in final response to their news (*voce quasi gaudentes*).[66] At
Chiemsee in the thirteenth century Mary Magdalene runs rejoicing
to sing to the two Disciples the famous *Victimae paschali*.[67]

Most frequent throughout the texts of the liturgical drama is the
rubrical requirement that characters cry out (*clamare*). In addition
to the *Daniel*, there are more than a dozen uses of *clamare*, and
their theatrical contexts reveal a range of emotional expressions. In
the thirteenth-century *Ludus Paschalis* from Tours, the Angel cries
out to the Marys "with an intense voice" (*alta voce clamat*): "Come!
Come! Come!"—see the empty Sepulcher.[68] In the Cathedral of Essen
in the fourteenth century, one of the Disciples announces the Resurrection from above in the organ loft—*clamabit sic*: "Christus Dominus surrexit."[69] Or in the thirteenth-century Greater Passion Play
from Benediktbeuern, Mary the Mother of Jesus weeps, crying out to
the other women.[70] In the *Daniel*, however, Balthasar cries out
(*clamare*) not in joy but in terror, shaken by the vision of the writing
Hand. Only here in the extant liturgical drama does one find this
fear-driven sense of *clamare*. The Beauvais song-school writers preferred the verb *exclamare* and used it in the *Daniel* three times.

These choices of words and their dramatic contexts in rubrics of
other liturgical dramas can expand and deepen the understanding of
specific actions and emotional expressions called for in the rubrics of
the Beauvais *Daniel*. In addition, when taken together they reveal
an unusually large range of vocal and gestural language demanded
of the actor-singers performing the roles. Overall one is struck by
the number of staging analogues that derive from the twelfth- and
thirteenth-century manuscripts—witnesses to a spirit of invention in
the drama that matched the opening of a powerful new era in the
history of music.

NOTES

[1] See Karl Young, *The Drama of the Medieval Church* (Oxford: Clarendon Press, 1933), II, 290–306; William L. Smoldon, *The Music of the Medieval Church Dramas*, ed. Cynthia Bourgeault (London: Oxford Univ. Press, 1980), pp. 234–35; Margot Fassler, "The Feast of Fools and *Danielis Ludus*: Popular Tradition in a Medieval Cathedral Play," in *Plainsong in the Age of Polyphony*, ed. Thomas Forrest Kelly (Cambridge: Cambridge Univ. Press, 1992), pp. 65–99. Attention to staging is, however, given in Fletcher Collins, Jr., *The Production of Medieval Church Music-Drama* (Charlottesville: Univ. Press of Virginia, 1972), pp. 242–55, which usefully provides reference to relevant examples from the visual arts.

In my quotations and translations from the play, I have followed the edition and translation in the present book.

[2] David Wulstan, Introd., *The Play of Daniel: A Mediaeval Liturgical Drama*, ed. W. L. Smoldon, revised by David Wulstan (Sutton: Plainsong and Mediaeval Music Soc., 1976), p. i.

[3] See ibid., p. i; Jerome Taylor, "Prophetic 'Play' and Symbolist 'Plot' in the Beauvais *Daniel*," *Comparative Drama*, 11 (1977), 191. Richard K. Emmerson, in another article in the present volume, argues for the likelihood of a later date.

[4] Stephen Murray, *Beauvais Cathedral: Architecture of Transcendence* (Princeton: Princeton Univ. Press, 1989), p. 11; André Louis Pierre, *Cathédrales de France: Arts-Techniques-Société* (Paris: Productions de Paris, 1962), p. 348.

[5] Murray, *Beauvais Cathedral*, figs. 3–5.

[6] Andrew Hughes, "Liturgical Drama: Falling Between the Disciplines," in *The Theatre of Medieval Europe: New Research in Early Drama*, ed. Eckehard Simon (Cambridge: Cambridge Univ. Press, 1991), p. 61.

[7] E. Martin Browne, Preface, in *The Play of Daniel*, ed. Noah Greenberg (New York: Oxford Univ. Press, 1959), p. vi.

[8] Nikos Psacharopolous, "Notes on Staging," in *The Play of Daniel*, ed. Greenberg, p. 112.

[9] Taylor, "Prophetic 'Play' and Symbolist 'Plot'," p. 201; Wulstan, in *The Play of Daniel*, ed. Smoldon, rev. Wulstan, p. iii.

[10] Émile Chami, "Chronique des fouilles médiévales en France," *Archéologie Médiévale*, 1 (1971), 280; hereafter abbreviated as Chami, "Chronique," *AM*, since the article was published in several parts. Translations from these articles are mine.

[11] Chami, "Chronique," *AM*, 6 (1976), 341.

[12] Taylor, "Prophetic 'Play' and Symbolist 'Plot'," p. 203. For the designation of Balthasar as a King of the Feast, a role normally taken by a subdeacon, see Fassler, "The Feast of Fools and *Danielis Ludus*," p. 88.

[13] See Fassler, "The Feast of Fools and *Danielis Ludus*," p. 71.

[14] Chami, "Chronique," *AM*, 1 (1971), 280.

[15] Murray, *Beauvais Cathedral*, fig. 31; Pierre, *Cathédrales de France*, p. 346.

[16] Chami, "Chronique," *AM*, 1 (1971), 280.

[17] Murray, *Beauvais Cathedral*, p. 11.

[18] Pierre, *Cathédrales de France*, p. 348.

[19] Chami, "Chronique," *AM*, 7 (1977), 261.

[20] Browne, Preface, p. vi.

[21] See John Stevens, "Medieval Drama," in *The New Grove Dictionary of Music and Musicians*, ed. Stanley Sadie (London: Macmillan, 1980), XII, 36–37.

[22] W. L. Smoldon, ed., *The Play of Daniel: A Mediaeval Liturgical Drama* (London: Faith Press, 1960), p. 3.

[23] See E. K. Chambers, *The Mediaeval Stage* (London: Oxford Univ. Press, 1903), I, 285–89.

[24] Wulstan, in *The Play of Daniel*, ed. Smoldon, revised Wulstan, p. i; Fassler, "The Feast of Fools and *Danielis Ludus*," pp. 65–99.

[25] Young, *The Drama of the Medieval Church*, II, 303.

[26] Fassler, "The Feast of Fools and *Danielis Ludus*," pp. 85–86.

[27] Young, *The Drama of the Medieval Church*, II, 486.

[28] Chami, "Chronique," *AM*, 3–4 (1973–74), 404.

[29] Chami, "Chronique," *AM*, 6 (1976), 340.

[30] See Young, *The Drama of the Medieval Church*, II, 302–03, and also Chambers, *The Mediaeval Stage*, II, 58–60.

[31] Young, *The Drama of the Medieval Church*, II, 303.

[32] Wulstan, in *The Play of Daniel*, ed. Smoldon, revised Wulstan, pp. ii.

[33] Young, *The Drama of the Medieval Church*, II, 304.

[34] Ibid., II, 302.

[35] C. Clifford Flanigan, "Medieval Latin Music-Drama," in *The Theatre of Medieval Europe*, ed. Simon, p. 37. Flanigan was referring in particular to the edition of the play prepared by Wulf Arlt, *Ein Festoffizium des Mittelalters aus Beauvais* (Cologne: Arno Volk, 1970), 2 vols.

[36] Susan Rankin, "Liturgical Drama," in *The Early Middle Ages to 1300*, ed. Richard Crocker and David Hiley, New Oxford of Music, 2 (Oxford: Oxford Univ. Press, 1990), p. 352.

[37] Smoldon, ed., *The Play of Daniel*, p. 13.

[38] See David G. Hughes, "Liturgical Polyphony at Beauvais in the Thirteenth Century," *Speculum*, 34 (1959), 184–200.

[39] Chami, "Chronique," *AM*, 1 (1971), 279.

[40] Chami, "Chronique," *AM*, 3–4 (1973–74), 403.

[41] Chami, "Chronique," *AM*, 6 (1976), 340.

[42] Young, *The Drama of the Medieval Church*, II, 69.

[43] Ibid., II, 371ff.

[44] Ibid., II, 199, 220, 344, 355; the plays are *The Raising of Lazarus, The Conversion of St. Paul, Iconia,* and *The Son of Getron.*

[45] Ibid., II, 267.

[46] Ibid., I, 578; *Lateinische Osterfeiern und Osterspiele,* ed. Walther Lipphardt, 9 vols. (Berlin: Walter de Gruyter, 1975–90), No. 360; hereafter designated as *LOO*.

[47] *LOO*, Nos. 746, 747 (Sion); Young, *The Drama of the Medieval Church*, I, 280, and *LOO*, Nos. 349–50 (Trier); Young, *The Drama of the Medieval Church*, II, 257, and *LOO*, Nos. 372–73 (Würzburg).

[48] Young, *The Drama of the Medieval Church*, I, 461, 693, and *LOO*, Nos. 812–13 (Rouen); Young, *The Drama of the Medieval Church*, I, 463, and *LOO*, No. 820 (Benediktbeuern); Young, *The Drama of the Medieval Church*, I, 481 (Padua *Peregrinus*).

[49] Young, *The Drama of the Medieval Church*, I, 468; *LOO*, No. 808.

[50] See David Bevington, *Medieval Drama* (Boston: Houghton Mifflin, 1975), pp. 137ff, for a suggestion concerning stage arrangement in a church. He proposes three raised platforms in the crossing (the nave, immediately in front of the east choir): the palace, Daniel's house, and the lions' den. "The palace is sumptuous and large, featuring a high throne for the king and a seat for Daniel. . . ." In his view the interior of the lion pit should be made visible and the lions should be played by human actors so that the audience can witness the moment when the counselors are "eaten immediately by the lions." He sees the Angel at the conclusion as appearing in "an elevated vantage point in the church." Further, he envisions the staging of "brilliant pageantry," with singers accompanied by harps, zithers, and drums: everywhere "purple garments" and "regal robes" as well as "sumptuous vessels" at King Balthasar's banquet.

David Wulstan has posited the following general schematic description concerning the way in which the architecture of the *Basse-Œuvre* may have been put to use as performance space for *The Play of Daniel*:

> Where the architecture of the building demanded it, mediaeval Liturgical Dramas seemed to make use of a stage, placed centrally, and flanked by the traditional *plateae* for the "good" and "bad" characters—Daniel's house stage right and the Lions' den at stage left. Simple sets might have been used at these two locations. The three thrones (for the Queen, King and Daniel) would dominate the stage; perhaps a canopy on which the writing could appear (as to the method, mediaeval ingenuity was no doubt a match for modern technology) would complete the set for the Royal palace. (Wulstan, in *The Play of Daniel*, ed. Smoldon, revised Wulstan, pp. 27–28)

This reconstruction strays far from the original rubrics of the *Daniel* and from staging information contained in other liturgical dramas. Moreover, *platea* is a term from the outdoor medieval drama referring to a neutral playing space. The notion of good characters at stage right and bad at stage left is a modern suggestion for outdoor medieval drama and based on scanty evidence; more likely bad characters would be placed to the north, the direction associated with the powers of darkness. It has been pointed out that the Gospel is read to the north as a challenge to those evil powers (see Clifford Davidson, "Space and Time in Medieval Drama," in *Word, Picture, and Spectacle*, Early Drama, Art, and Music, Monograph Ser. 5 [Kalamazoo: Medieval Institute Publications, 1984], p. 44). In the rubrics of the *Daniel* no throne is mentioned for the Queen; Daniel sits next to the King, but, again, no throne is noted. And the canopy with the mysterious writing is made out of whole cloth.

[51] Fassler, "The Feast of Fools and *Danielis Ludus*," pp. 91–92. The *Prose of the Ass* is contained in the same manuscript in which *The Play of Daniel* appears (Egerton MS. 2615, fols. 1–2, 43–44); see Henry Copley Greene, "The Song of the Ass," *Speculum*, 6 (1931), 534–49, and also Young, *The Drama of the Medieval Church*, II, 303.

[52] Young, *The Drama of the Medieval Church*, II, 281.

[53] Ibid., II, 180, and I, 462; *LOO*, No. 812.

[54] *Medieval Drama*, ed. Bevington, p. 112.

[55] The word *quasi*, which delineates this border between ritual and drama in performance, harks back to the earliest example of the liturgical drama in the tenth century; in the *Visitatio Sepulchri* in the *Regularis Concordia*, the Marys "come to the place of the [Easter] sepulchre" with hesitation "in imitation of those seeking for something [*pedetemptim ad similitudinem querentium*]. For these things are done in order to imitate [*Aguntur enim hec ad imitationem*] the angel seated on the tomb and the women coming with spices in order to anoint the body of Jesus" (quoted by Pamela Sheingorn, *The Easter Sepulchre in England*, Early Drama, Art, and Music, Reference Ser. 5 [Kalamazoo: Medieval Institute Publications, 1987], pp. 20–23).

[56] Young, *The Drama of the Medieval Church*, I, 472; *LOO*, No. 817.

[57] Young, *The Drama of the Medieval Church*, I, 514, and II, 200, 355.

[58] Young, *The Drama of the Medieval Church*, II, 259.

[59] Ibid., II, 85, 89.

[60] For an example of David in prayer with his hands extended and palms out—a miniature in the *Silos Bible*—see Collins, *Production*, fig. 65. The gesture is likely to have had a long history; see the fourth-century relief in a Roman sarcophagus illustrated by Gertrud Schiller, *Christian Iconography*, trans. Janet Seligman (Greenwich, Conn.: New York Graphic Soc., 1971), I, fig. 249. On the gesture for prayer with hands joined (*junctus manibus*), see Lynn White, Jr., "Medieval Borrowings from Further Asia," in *Medieval and Renaissance Studies 5*, ed. O. B. Hardison, Jr. (Chapel Hill: Univ. of North Carolina Press, 1971), p. 17, citing Gerhart B. Ladner, "The Gestures of Prayer in Papal Iconography of the Thirteenth and Fourteenth Centuries," in *Didascaliae: Studies in Honor of Anselm M. Albareda*, ed. S. Prete (New York, 1961), pp. 247–75.

[61] Young, *The Drama of the Medieval Church*, I, 388; *LOO*, No. 797.

[62] Young, *The Drama of the Medieval Church*, II, 87.

[63] Ibid., I, 384, 418–19; *LOO*, Nos. 770, 825.

[64] Young, *The Drama of the Medieval Church*, I, 408; *LOO*, No. 771.

[65] Young, *The Drama of the Medieval Church*, II, 110.

[66] Ibid., I, 350; *LOO*, No. 772.

[67] *LOO*, No. 782.

[68] Young, *The Drama of the Medieval Church*, I, 442; *LOO*, No. 824.

[69] Young, *The Drama of the Medieval Church*, I, 334–35; *LOO*, No. 564.

[70] Young, *The Drama of the Medieval Church*, I, 530.

Divine Judgment and Local Ideology in the Beauvais *Ludus Danielis*

Richard K. Emmerson

In his survey of scholarship on "Medieval Latin Music-Drama," C. Clifford Flanigan noted that "The *Ludus Danielis* from the cathedral school at Beauvais is one of the best known of all Latin music-dramas, yet strangely there has been little written about it. . . ."[1] Important progress in that direction has been made by Margot Fassler, whose essay on "The Feast of Fools and *Danielis Ludus*" is an excellent examination of the play within its liturgical and musical contexts.[2] My essay, building upon Fassler's work, seeks to reconceive the play by moving beyond its liturgical setting to examine its exegetical, historical, and ideological contexts. By ideology I do not mean to suggest the "false consciousness" that is assumed by the Marxist paradigm of base/superstructure but rather a much more fluid "thought-system" that includes interconnected religious, political, and social ideas and beliefs that a particular group of persons at a particular time and place consider "a crucial part of what it is to be themselves."[3] An ideological thought-system, although a form of discourse, is based on largely unexamined assumptions that its particular interpretive community assumes to be "natural," "normal," "obvious," that which "goes without saying."[4] This notion of ideology accounts for the ways a cultural work such as the *Ludus Danielis* both accumulates meaning within larger universalizing ("timeless") frameworks such as twelfth-century liturgical and historical structures and manifests significance for a particular community at a particular historical moment ("timeliness"). My approach seeks to follow Flanigan's summons that we understand medieval plays "as monuments of social practices concerned with establishing a world view in specific communities at definite moments in history" and that we recognize that these texts represent "communal actions un-

33

dertaken because they had social, economic, or cultural utility."[5]

Specifically, this essay will begin by surveying the place of the biblical book of *Daniel* in medieval exegesis and describing its role within the schema that characterize the growing awareness of history in the high Middle Ages. The goal will be to examine how the *Ludus Danielis* stages crucial moments within the Christian understanding of salvation history to represent a "timeless" sense of divine judgments and their relationship to the people of God throughout history. The essay will next focus on twelfth- and early thirteenth-century political and ecclesiastic developments to trace some features of the ideology of Beauvais and to suggest how the *Ludus Danielis* may be understood within this local context. In moving beyond the liturgical and exegetical—that is, beyond those aspects of early medieval drama that scholars have tended to emphasize as universalizing the theatrical within the grand schemes of liturgical ritual and salvation history—the essay investigates the particular historicity of this rich text to show how it both reflects and informs the local ideology of Beauvais, how, in other words, the play is also particularly "timely" for the interpretive community gathered in Beauvais.

Just as the extravagant Gothic cathedral of Beauvais sought to monumentalize the increased prosperity and power of its count-bishop and his role as an independent yet faithful peer of the realm, so the rich liturgical manuscript, copied around 1230 at a time when the rebuilding of the cathedral was in its very early stages, became a textualized counterpart of the cathedral, inscribing the local traditions of Beauvais.[6] My approach combines a more traditional exegetical reading of the play with an understanding that such a reading has local import, best understood when approaching the play as a cultic performance that helped develop an ecclesiastical ideology of local theocracy that was crucial to Beauvais in the later twelfth and early thirteenth centuries. This theocratic thought system stood as a bulwark against the growing centralizing power of Paris, which was then being transformed, as John Baldwin notes, into "the true capital of the kingdom."[7] It was underscored as a contrast to the hegemonic claims of the reinvigorated Capetian dynasty, which during this period was not only threatening the aristocratic power of the nobility but also appropriating a religious function for itself, as evident in the royal title, *rex christianissimus* ("most Christian king").[8] The developing Parisian ideology of *royal* theocracy is perhaps best exemplified by the letter Suger, Abbot of St. Denis (1122–51), sent to the bishop, chapter, and people of Beauvais on behalf of Louis VII (1137–80), who is boldly described as "the King of kings" as well as "the king of the Franks."[9] The steady and seemingly inevitable ascendancy of the French monarchy continued during the long reign of Louis VII's son, Philip II ("Augustus," 1180–1223), and culminated during the "saintly" reign of Louis IX (1226–70), the grandson of Philip Augustus, who reigned when the *Ludus Danielis* was given its present manuscript form.[10]

I

Daniel in Medieval Exegesis. Daniel, in the Hebrew Bible, is a mixture of two literary genres, with roughly half of the book devoted to each genre.[11] The first six chapters and the apocryphal additions of chapters 13 and 14 are popular folktale-like narratives that exemplify the foolish pride of the Babylonian kings and their humbling before the powerful God of Israel. The motif that regulates the trajectory of these narratives is the certainty that the absolute power of the eternal God will control temporal affairs and will, when appropriate, unravel what is mysterious to the finite human understanding: "Blessed be the name of the Lord from eternity and for evermore: for wisdom and fortitude are his. And he changeth times and ages: taketh away kingdoms and establisheth them, giveth wisdom to the wise, and knowledge to them that have understanding. He revealeth deep and hidden things, and knoweth what is in darkness: and light is with him" (*Dan.* 2.20–22).[12]

Throughout, the Babylonian kings, even when the truth is revealed to them by God's prophet, tend to be arrogant and unteachable. Therefore, Nebuchadnezzar must ultimately be punished by being driven from Babylon into the fields where he "did eat grass like an ox, and his body was wet with the dew of heaven: till his hairs grew like the feathers of eagles, and his nails like birds' claws" (*Dan.* 4.30).[13] And Belshazzar must be overthrown by Darius the Mede (*Dan.* 5.31). In medieval exegesis these stories came to symbolize not only the punishment of the wicked but also God's protection of the faithful. One of the most memorable of these narratives is the story of the three young Hebrews exiled in Babylon whose faith in their unseen heavenly God is so firm that they are willing to face the fiery furnace rather than to worship the earthly idol set before their eyes by Nebuchadnezzar (*Dan.* 3). Their salvation in the furnace is cited by Bernard of Clairvaux in the twelfth century as an example of God's continuing protection of the faithful. Noting that the three Hebrews were joined in the furnace by a fourth "like the Son of God" (*Dan.* 3.92), Bernard comments: "Why should we tremble, why should we hesitate, why flee this furnace? The fire rages, but the Lord is with us in tribulation."[14]

The youth Daniel, noted for his wisdom and faithfulness, plays a prominent role throughout the book. In contrast to the soothsayers and magi of Babylon, Daniel, who is called their "colleague" (*Dan.* 4.5), is able to interpret God's judgments revealed through several enigmatic dreams (*Dan.* 2.31–46, 4.7–24) and by the ominous handwriting on the wall (*Dan.* 5.5, 25–29). He is always portrayed as wise and as a true prophet in contrast to the pseudo "wise men" and diviners. Through "a vision in the night" (*Dan.* 2.19), for example, God reveals to Daniel both the dream that Nebuchadnezzar had forgotten and its interpretation; the prophet is thus able to save from death the Chaldean diviners and magicians as well as the Hebrew youths. As an exile from the theocratic kingdom of Israel centered in the temple and based in prayer, Daniel is a man of prayer in Babylon, a land of idolatry. Even when the envious royal counsellors hatch a plot to trap Daniel by ruling that prayer to any but Darius should be punishable by death, the prophet remains faithful: "Now when Daniel knew this, that is to say, that the law was made, he went into his house: and opening the windows in his upper chamber towards Jerusalem, he knelt down three times a day, and adored, and gave thanks before his God, as he had been accustomed to do before" (*Dan.* 6.10). Daniel continues to witness for the God of Israel when he braves the lions' den (*Dan.* 6.16–23)—an act which leads Darius to acknowledge Yahweh as "the living and eternal God for ever: and his kingdom shall not be destroyed, and his power shall be for ever" (*Dan.* 6.26).

The apocryphal additions to the Hebrew book continue to portray Daniel's wisdom and judgment, whether in opposition to the Jewish elders or to the Babylonian priests. Even as a young boy, Daniel is a wise judge. He is raised up by God to expose the two judges who, driven by the evils of Babylon (*Dan.* 13:5), falsely accuse Susanna of adultery. He is also a trickster-like subversive who challenges the priests of Bel, proving their trickery and destroying the idol of Bel (*Dan.* 14.10–21). When he also destroys the dragon worshipped by the Babylonians (*Dan.* 14.26), he is again thrown to the lions, where he is fed by the prophet Habakkuk, who is carried by an Angel from Judea to Babylon and back (*Dan.* 14.32–38). The *Ludus Danielis* conflates this apocryphal scene with the earlier account of Daniel in the lions' den.

Most medieval exegesis of *Daniel* follows Jerome's authoritative commentary. Composed in 407, it was not superseded in the Middle Ages.[15] Jerome, stressing the historicity of the folkloric narratives, Daniel's youth, and the prophet's peculiar role in the court of the Babylonian kings, notes that, unlike the Babylonian magi, Daniel "spoke by the Spirit of God."[16] But Jerome also stresses that Daniel continued to honor the Babylonian and Persian kings and avoided openly opposing secular authority even when following the commands of God and remaining the faithful man of prayer.[17] Although Jerome discounts the canonicity of the apocryphal chapters appended to the Hebrew book, the medieval tradition does embrace the story of Susanna and particularly Daniel's role as a divinely inspired and resourceful judge and a model of just judgment—"A Daniel come to judgment," in Shylock's words.[18] In addition to the praise of Daniel by Jerome, during the twelfth century Daniel's symbolic currency was further inflated. He was understood not only as a faithful man of prayer and wise judge but also as a model of contemplation, as a symbol of the celibacy of the Church, and as the representative of hope in the traditional triad of faith, hope, and charity.[19] He was also understood as the model interpreter of dreams, a role that led to the *Somniale Danielis*, a popular handbook of dream interpretation.[20] Further, to Rupert of Deutz, who interprets his name to signify "iudicium Dei" ("judgment of God"), Daniel was an Old Testament type of Christ.[21]

The second half of the book of *Daniel* includes a series of esoteric apocalyptic visions that established Daniel's fame as a prophet as well as an interpreter of dreams. In the biblical tradition and in

medieval exegesis Daniel thus became an authoritative apocalyptic
visionary, a position underscored by Jesus, who cites Daniel in his
own enigmatic apocalyptic pronouncements: "And therefore when
you shall see the abomination of desolation, which was spoken of by
Daniel the prophet, standing in the holy place: he that readeth let
him understand" (*Matt.* 24.15). In medieval exegesis Daniel's visions
were understood as outlining, first, a chronology of world empires
during the fifth age of world history; and, second, as prophesying the
very end of the sixth age of world history, specifically the rise and
career of Antichrist. The vision of the four beasts (*Dan.* 7.1–14), for
example, was interpreted to represent the four empires that would
dominate the fifth age of world history: Babylon, Medo-Persia,
Greece, and Rome.[22] And the "little horn" that springs from the
midst of the fourth beast's ten horns (*Dan.* 7.8) was early identified
as symbolizing Antichrist, "one of the human race, in whom Satan
will wholly take up his residence in bodily form."[23] The role of
Daniel as wise interpreter and judge was thus reinforced by his
status as prophet of the end of both the fifth and the sixth ages of
world history—that is, as prophet of both the first and the second
coming of Christ. Hence Daniel appears as a prophet of the Nativity
in the Towneley *Play of the Prophets* and the N-Town *Play of the
Root of Jesse*, for example, and as a prophet of the last days in the
Chester *Prophets of Antichrist*. He is also cited in the Chester *Coming of Antichrist*.[24]

Daniel's role as prophet of the Nativity was so important that he
was even credited as the teacher of other prophets. According to
Martin of Léon, Virgil, whose Fourth Eclogue was read as a prophecy of the birth of Christ, supposedly learned of this divine event
from Daniel.[25] Daniel's time prophecies—those focusing on various
enumerated "days" and "weeks"—were interpreted as prophesying
the end of the special status of the children of Israel as Yahweh's
chosen people. The enigmatic vision during the first year of Darius'
reign (*Dan.* 9.1) is repeatedly cited. Gabriel appears to Daniel to explain that "Seventy weeks are shortened upon thy people, and upon
thy holy city, that transgression may be finished, and sin may have
an end, and iniquity may be abolished; and everlasting justice may
be brought; and vision and prophecy may be fulfilled; and the saint
of saints may be anointed" (*Dan.* 9.24). The specificity of the seventy

weeks led Augustine to credit Daniel with dating the advent and life of Christ.[26] This interpretation of the seventy weeks probably entered the dramatic tradition through the pseudo-Augustinian sermon *Contra Judaeos, Paganos, et Arianos* in which Daniel appears to prophesy: "Cum venerit, inquit, Sanctus Sanctorum, cessabit unctio" ("When the Holy of Holies comes, he says, the anointing shall cease").[27]

Scholars have long debated the relationship of the *Ludus Danielis* to the Pseudo-Augustinian sermon and the *Ordo prophetarum*.[28] I agree with the scholarly consensus that the play is unlikely to be a mere elaboration of the few lines spoken by the prophet in the *ordo*, even through the mediation of the Daniel play by Hilarius.[29] To begin with, as Jerome Taylor has shown, liturgical readings from Daniel are important throughout the season of Advent—readings not limited to Daniel's prophecy of the Holy of Holies.[30] The exegetical tradition, furthermore, and the role of the prophet provided many sources for such biblical drama as well as a firm rationale for commemorating this remarkable hero. Added to the rich symbolism attached to Daniel is his enduring youth—for it is no matter that he served kings ranging over several generations—he is consistently portrayed as a "juventus" ("young man") and "adolescens" ("youth") and is therefore a particularly appropriate model for the youth of Beauvais.[31] Rather than searching for the textual origins of the play, then, or even focusing primarily on its relationship to its companion play, we should investigate its function as a social practice within the ritual community of Beauvais cathedral.

II

The Function of the Ludus Danielis. Clearly one purpose of the play is to commemorate the events related to the Nativity of Christ. This is true whether the play was performed "after matins before the midnight Mass of Christmas," as Taylor suggests, or on the Feast of the Circumcision (1 January) as assumed by most commentators—an occasion that would associate the *Ludus Danielis* with its companion texts in the Egerton manuscript.[32] The commemorative function is evident at the play's conclusion, for example, when Daniel speaks his most famous prophecy (ll. 385–88), an Angel suddenly appears to proclaim, "natus est Christus" ("Christ is born" [l. 390]), and the *cantores* begin the *Te Deum laudamus*. Earlier, the *conductus* for the Queen alludes to "hac die . . . sollempni" ("this most solemn day" [l. 192]), suggesting a festive day, and, when conducting Daniel to Darius, the *legati* sing in praise of the "natalis sollempnia" ("the solemn feast of the Nativity" [l. 270]), allude to Daniel's prophecy of the cessation of the anointing (l. 274), and conclude, "Ergo sit laus Dei verbo genito de virgine" ("Therefore praise be to the Word of God, born of the Virgin" [l. 284]). In all of these passages, the songs celebrate the season rather than forwarding the dramatic narrative.[33]

Yet the play passes over one important scene from the book of *Daniel* that had strong prophetic associations with the Nativity: the story of the three Hebrews in the fiery furnace. After Nebuchadnezzar has the three youths bound and thrown into the furnace, he is astonished to see four men walking through the flames (*Dan.* 3. 91–92). The pseudo-Augustinian sermon treats Nebuchadnezzar's response to the fourth figure in the furnace as a Christological prophecy:

> *Nonne*, inquit, *tres uiros misimus in fornace ligatos?* Et aiunt ei: *Vere, rex. Ecce*, inquit, *ego uideo quatuor uiros solutos deambulantes in medio ignis, et corruptio nulla est in eis, et aspectus quarti similis est Filio Dei.*[34]

> (*Did we not*, he says, *throw three men bound into the furnace?* And they to him: *Truly, king. Behold*, he says, *I see four men loose walking in the midst of the fire, and there is no corruption in them, and the appearance of the fourth is like the Son of God*.)

This scene, furthermore, is included in other prophetic plays, including the twelfth-century *Ordo repraesentationis Adae* and the fourteenth-century Rouen *Procession of the Prophets*. The Rouen *Prophets* stages a fiery furnace in the center of the nave and calls for an idol and seat for Nebuchadnezzar.[35] Had the primary purpose of the *Ludus Danielis* been to commemorate the Nativity by developing the various Christological prophecies in the book of *Daniel*, the three Hebrews and Nebuchadnezzar's prophecy of the Son of God would have been effective components of the play composed and produced by the youth of Beauvais.

In fact, not only does the play not stage this important narrative, but it actually devotes only a relatively small portion of its lines and little of its action to prophecies of the Nativity. A quick count reveals that the traditional materials associated with Christmas are the focus of only about five percent of the play. It is thus worthwhile to focus on the "excess" of the *Ludus Danielis*, that is, on what seems to be the extravagant supplementarity of most of its performance. Focusing on the roughly 95% of the play that does not explicitly celebrate the Christmas season will make clear that, once we bracket the play's liturgical setting and examine its "social utility," the dramatic action foregrounds other themes equally important to the twelfth-century understanding of Daniel and, more specifically, relevant to the local ideology of Beauvais.

While fulfilling a liturgical role, the *Ludus Danielis* also fulfills a political one; while celebrating the Christmas season it also underscores the proper relation between secular and sacred authority, an issue central to the theocratic beliefs of Beauvais. This relationship is figured by the repeated contrasts that the action and language of the play draw between Jerusalem and Babylon and between Daniel as man of God, representing the theocratic state of Israel in exile, and the royal figures of Balthasar (the Latin form of the name Belshazzar adopted in the play) and Darius and their magi, princes, and satraps, representing the dominant and apparently all-powerful monarchy. The play stages the controlling power of the monarchy by treating the royal personages with great respect, repeating the formula, "Rex, in eternum vive" ("King, live forever") throughout, even near its conclusion, when Daniel, in the lions' den, recognizes Darius (l. 375). But that power is questioned as the play repeatedly suggests the proper relationship between monarch and man of God, reestablishing the divinely ordained order whenever it is threatened.

This relationship is especially evident in the play's linking of Daniel's prophecies to various moments of "judgment." The first prophecy foregrounded by the play's action, the enigmatic handwriting on the wall, is interpreted by Daniel as a specific divine judgment on Balthasar. This prophecy is fulfilled almost immediately, when Darius arrives on stage and his followers, by means of a dumb show, carry out the judgment of God by executing Balthasar: "*Antequam perveniat Rex ad solium suum duo precurrentes expellent*

Balthasar quasi interficientes eum. Tunc sedente Dario Rege in maiestate sua, Curia exclamabit: Rex in eternum vive" (*"Before the King reaches his throne, two men running ahead drive out Balthasar, as if killing him. Then, when King Darius is seated in majesty, the court exclaims:* King, live forever" [l. 246]). The second prophecy, Daniel's famous prophecy regarding the end of the anointing, is the focus of most commentators who emphasize the play's function within the liturgy of the Christmas season. It is usually interpreted as a divine judgment on the Jews: "Cessat regni Iudeorum contumax potentia" ("The stubborn power of the kingdom of the Jews ceases" [l. 275]). This prophecy is not fulfilled immediately, but only at the play's conclusion, when Daniel formally delivers his prophecy (ll. 385–88) and the Angel suddenly appears to announce the birth of Christ, "dominator orbis" ("Ruler of the world" [l. 390]).

The play's third "prophecy" is not explicit, but is, I believe, nevertheless significant. It is implicit in Daniel's well-established role as apocalyptic visionary, the Queen's praise of Daniel's prophetic powers (ll. 102–09), and the allusions to Daniel's earlier dealings with Nebuchadnezzar (ll. 151–54) and the king's humiliation when "Grass became his food" (l. 162). This is a prophecy that assumes Babylon's symbolic status as the ultimate demonic city and the representative of evil during the Last Days.[36] It is a prophecy of the Last Judgment, implied by Daniel's role as prophet of Christ's second as well as first advent.[37] But the action of the *Ludus Danielis* does not move into the apocalyptic future. The fulfillment of this third, implied, prophecy is not staged but presented typologically through the story of Daniel in the lions' den. The Babylonian pit is closely connected to death, just as in the *Apocalypse* Babylon symbolizes hell and is linked to the city of man at the end of the world.[38] In this metaphorical hell, Daniel is protected by the Angel, fed by the prophet Habakkuk, and then ultimately freed to resume his role as advisor to Darius. The entire scene, specifically the Angel's intervention and Daniel's response to Habakkuk ("Recordatus es mei Domine" ["Lord, you have remembered me"], l. 370), is powerfully reminiscent of the protection of God expected by the faithful at Doomsday and their grateful recognition of that protection. In this typologically staged prophecy, Daniel's rising from the pit then symbolizes both the resurrection of the faithful at Doomsday as well as the Harrowing of Hell—a well established type of the Last Judgment.[39] If Daniel here symbolizes the righteous saved, then the final judgment on—and punishment of—Darius' counsellors typologically prefigures the traditional separation of good and evil and punishment of the damned at Doomsday.[40]

The triple set of prophecies in the *Ludus Danielis* and the judgments enacted over time underscore the importance of historical models for the understanding of the play. The conflation of these crucial events of salvation history into the dramatic narrative resembles the "nonlinear sense of time, an 'all time,' . . ." that Margot Fassler, in an essay on the *Play of Adam*, describes as characteristic of twelfth-century liturgical art: "it is an art with a view of time, a time wherein all events can be seen at once, placed one on top of the other in layers, lined up, focused, and explained through Christ."[41] Fassler connects these various layers of time to the four levels of biblical interpretation that characterized twelfth-century exegesis. Although I doubt that either the *Adam* or *Daniel* develops these "levels" systematically, they do provide a useful heuristic for understanding the ways in which both plays deal with time since this hermeneutic model is clearly based on a peculiarly medieval Christian sense of history.

The prophecies and judgments in the *Ludus Danielis*, for example, correspond rather neatly to the various interpretive "levels." The handwriting on the wall and the judgment on Balthasar represent the first level, the literal or historical, which is both set and fulfilled in the Old Testament past. The second or allegorical level is evident in Daniel's prophecy regarding the Holy of Holies. It is fulfilled by the birth of Christ, which is prefigured in the Old Testament past, fulfilled in the New Testament past, and commemorated during the liturgical season of Christmas. The apocalyptic prophecies associated with Daniel and typified by the judgment on the Satraps thrown to the lions represent the fourth, anagogical level, which is associated with Christian eschatology. Set in the Old Testament past and prefigured by Christ during the Harrowing of Hell in the New Testament past, this prophecy is to be fulfilled in the future at Doomsday.

What is missing in this sketch, of course, is the third level, the tropological or moral. Although like the others set in the past, its

fulfillment must be enacted in the present of the play's performance.
It is also an implied prophecy and judgment, this time aimed
directly at the play's audience, including not only personages of
Beauvais but also, as the play notes, "those who are from far
away."[42] It is here that the play, while still calling to mind various
historical moments of divine judgment and the other levels of interpretation, models the proper relationship of secular and religious
authority. It is here that the play underscores for the audience the
local theocratic ideology of Beauvais. It is here, it seems to me, that
the *Ludus Danielis* becomes a prophecy, suggesting a judgment on
any secular power that fails to respect the authority of God and
God's ministers in the here and now. It is here that the timeless becomes timely.

III

The Ludus Danielis *and the Local Ideology of Beauvais.* Fassler
has argued that the *Ludus Danielis* represents an attempt to reform
the Circumcision Office of Beauvais Cathedral and that it thus is
best understood as a play composed for the Feast of Fools. I find this
argument compelling but not sufficient for interpretive purposes, because it does not address the play's ideological level. There are many
ways to reform the Circumcision Office, many festive ways to celebrate the Feast of Fools. But, specifically, why did Beauvais respond
to this reformist impulse with the *Ludus Danielis*? For the remainder of this essay, I wish to investigate how it matters that the play
was composed at Beauvais Cathedral. Here, then, I disagree with
Fassler, who states that "the fact that *Daniel* was, like the Circumcision Office contained in the same manuscript, put together at
Beauvais Cathedral really says very little about the work itself."[43] In
fact, I think the play both reflected and helped to strengthen a local
ideology that is of particular importance to Beauvais—to its count-
bishop, chapter, and students—and that it is crucial for our interpretation of the play that it was "put together at Beauvais cathedral." I
thus will focus on what Rainer Warning identifies as "the decisive
question" for the study of religious drama, "the institutional setting
to which it stood witness."[44]

I recognize the difficulties of deciphering the ideological level of any work of literature since by definition ideology is that which "goes without saying." The task is made even more daunting in the case of the *Ludus Danielis*, for it is difficult to date the play more accurately than within the ninety years between 1140 and 1230.[45] My hunch is that it dates from the 1160's or 1170's, when Ralph of Beauvais, an Englishman and, like Hilarius, a student of Abelard, taught at Beauvais. He was a famous *auctoritas* in classical as well as religious literature: "vir tam in divinis quam in saecularibus litteris eruditus" ("a man learned as much in divine as in secular letters").[46] Although I make no claim for his authorship, Ralph seems a likely candidate for the teacher of the "iuventus" (l. 4) credited with the play's composition in its opening lines.

Whatever the date for the composition of the play, it can be contextualized by outlining some historical developments during this period that provide clues to the ideology of Beauvais, which I have been characterizing as "theocratic." Developing during the twelfth century, this ideology assumed and bolstered the local claims, rights, and responsibilities of a county-bishopric that had for long, in Stephen Murray's words, "constituted a strategically important buffer zone between the royal domain and the potentially hostile county of Flanders and duchy of Normandy to the north." It was ruled, furthermore, by bishop-counts who became vassals of the king in 1015. They were often closely associated with the royal family. For example, Bishop Henry of France (1148–62) was the brother of Louis VII, and Bishop Philip of Dreux (1175–1217) was the cousin of Philip Augustus. According to Murray, Philip of Dreux was "the very epitome of the loyal bishop-warrior."[47] One of the most powerful bishops, Miles of Nanteuil (1217–34), was very close to Louis VIII (1223–26) and attended the king on his deathbed.[48]

Peers of the realm, the bishop-counts of Beauvais were supportive counsellors of the king, yet they jealously maintained their independence from Paris and, along with the cathedral chapter, protected their many hard-won and long-standing local rights.[49] As early as 1100, for example, the cathedral chapter complained to Pope Paschal II to prevent Philip I (1060–1108) from installing Stephen de Garlande, the king's chancellor, as bishop. In fact, Beauvais-Paris relations were often stormy. Philip I, who quarreled with Bishop Guy of Beauvais (1063–84), exiled the bishop, pillaged church lands, and even sold the plate of the cathedral.[50] It seems likely that the audience of the *Ludus Danielis* would recall this historical incident involving the sacred objects of Beauvais Cathedral when witnessing Balthasar's command to "Bring for my use the vessels/ My father took from the temple" (ll. 37–38) and when listening to the extended sequence of the Satraps, who focus on the vessels stolen from the Temple in Jerusalem (ll. 46–60).

The count-bishop was often caught between his local obligations to Beauvais and its chapter and his national duties to Paris and its king. If, for example, the bishop was not sufficiently protective of local rights, the chapter would complain vociferously, as it did against Bishop Philip of Dreux for not defending the rights of the cathedral against Philip Augustus: "My Lord, you know perfectly well that a certain count freely gave the county of Beauvais to the church of Saint Peter. You and your predecessors have held it until now with such a franchise that the king of France did not have the right to publish his orders or prohibitions in Beauvais, and could neither seize nor arrest. However, you have encouraged the king, our seigneur, to seize and hold our rents, our houses. . . ."[51] Yet, as late as 1235, the barons and councillors of Louis IX met at St. Denis to discuss the bishop of Beauvais, who was included among those churchmen who had rebelled against the king by refusing "to recognize the jurisdiction of the king's Court over the temporalities."[52] The issue of judicial jurisdiction remained a major source of contention between Beauvais and Paris.

This sometimes three-way power struggle between bishop and chapter, on the one hand, and bishop and king, on the other, was further complicated by the growing power of the commune of Beauvais, which was founded about 1099. Particularly noted for its turbulence, the commune jealously guarded its rights.[53] Encouraged by Louis VI (1108–37), these rights were confirmed in a charter issued by Louis VII in 1144. The communal rights were guaranteed by the monarchy so that the insurrection of the commune in 1232–33 was used by the queen mother, Blanche of Castille, and the young Louis IX as an excuse to intervene in city affairs and re-establish royal power in Beauvais. They took over the bishop's palace, set up their own court, and demanded payments from Miles of Nanteuil, one of Beauvais' most outspoken bishop-counts, who retaliated by imposing an interdict.[54]

David Bevington has noted that the lines in the play that praise the Babylonian Queen (ll. 181–94) "suggest a comparison of the queen to a royal member of the play's original audience."[55] This suggestion is plausible because, compared to the three verses devoted to the Queen in the biblical account (*Dan.* 5.10–12), the play definitely emphasizes her role. She is always portrayed positively and is not implicated in Balthasar's blasphemous feast. She is, furthermore, solemnly led away before Darius appears so that she is not associated with the execution of Balthasar. She is "prudens" (l. 81), the single representative of native wisdom in Babylon and its only memory of God's prophet. Her status in the play thus deserves attention; if Bevington is right, it would be enormously useful to identify a member of the audience with whom she is being compared.

One possible candidate is Adelaide of Savoy, queen of Louis VI. Her intervention in the affairs of Beauvais and her role in smoothing the relations between bishop and king certainly qualify her for such praise. Soon after his election as bishop in 1148, Henry of France fought with his brother, King Louis VII, who prepared an army to march against Beauvais. The king was dissuaded, according to John of Salisbury, by the intervention of Adelaide, mother of the quarreling brothers. In his *Historia pontificalis* John of Salisbury notes that "within a short time there was such strife between the brothers that the king summoned an army and was hastening to annihilate Beauvais when prudent advisers—Jocelin bishop of Soisson and Suger abbot of St. Denis—and *Queen Adelaide most of all*, urged the bishop to be less reckless and made peace between the brothers."[56] If the play does celebrate Adelaide for her good advice to her sons, its association of the French queen mother with the biblical queen who describes Daniel's prophetic powers to Balthasar (ll. 102–09) would be in accord with the exegetical tradition. For example, Jerome, explaining how the queen could know about Daniel and previous events unknown to Balthasar, argues that the queen was not Balthasar's wife but either his mother or grandmother.[57]

There are, of course, other candidates for the Queen who is praised in the play, including Adele of Champagne, the third wife of Louis VII, and the queen who finally gave him the male heir he so desperately sought.[58] The comparison of Balthasar's Queen to the good wife of *Proverbs* 31 (ll. 181–82)—a comparison absent in the version by Hilarius—may even celebrate their wedding in 1160.[59] The reference to the "rich spoils" (l. 186) given by the good wife may also allude to the birth of their son, the future Philip Augustus, in 1165.[60] Interestingly, later royal historiography came to understand Philip's birth as a heavenly gift. A miniature from an early copy of the *Grandes Chroniques de France*, for example, portrays Christ, emerging from a cloud, presenting a crowned child to Louis VII and Adele.[61]

Perhaps it is just as well that we cannot identify with certainty a royal figure in the audience or a particular occasion for the play's first performance because we might fall to the temptation to build an interpretation on the foundation of this one sense of the "original" when, in fact, the play would have a continuing significance for its interpretive community throughout the late twelfth and early thirteenth centuries. The ideology of Beauvais was developing throughout this period and leading to the grand designs of the Gothic Cathedral of St. Pierre, when the play was finally inscribed, along with its rich accompanying liturgical texts, in its present manuscript form. However one reads the praise of the Queen in the *Ludus Danielis*, there is no question that the play should be read within the context of the powerful local ideology of Beauvais. The man of God—the representative of the theocracy of Jerusalem, the exile within the royal city of Babylon, the wise judge of Susanna (ll. 279–81)—correlates with the complex role of the Beauvais bishop-counts, faithful counsellors to the kings of France and judges within their theocratically ruled jurisdiction. Just as Daniel was the faithful counsellor to Balthasar and Darius, yet was ultimately beholden only to God, so the theocratic ideology of Beauvais supports the secular role of the bishop-count who, although a peer of the realm, is ultimately beholden only to God.

Throughout, the language and action of the play repeatedly contrasts the royal personages to the divinely inspired prophet and judge. This necessity to draw a contrast between secular authority, which is not condemned but is clearly limited, may explain why the play does not stage the story of the three youths thrown into the fiery furnace—a story that, as we have seen, is associated with

Christological prophecy through Nebuchadnezzar's prophetic recognition of the fourth youth as the Son of God. The *Ludus Danielis* may elide this prophecy because it does not countenance any prophetic role for a king since that role would imply a religious function for the secular monarch. It would support the theocratic claims of Paris and challenge the unique theocratic status of Beauvais. Instead, although the play's ceremonial features focus on the Babylonian kings to a great extent and in rich detail, assuming that the community of Beauvais associates itself with Daniel and the God of Daniel, the royal characters are figured as the "other" who stand not only in contrast to Jerusalem but also to the Beauvais community. At the ideological level, then, Babylon as royal city is implicitly associated with Paris and its growing hegemony over its neighbors. Interestingly, this symbolic association was made during this period, but in a different context, by Bernard of Clairvaux, a close associate of Bishop Henry of France. Bernard advised the masters and students of Paris to "Flee from the midst of this Babylon, flee and save your souls."[62]

But it is important to realize that the play does not condemn secular power as intrinsically evil and, unlike the Herod plays, does not demonize the royal figures, even the condemned Balthasar, who responds honorably when he receives Daniel's interpretation of the handwriting on the wall. In representing Balthasar and Darius, the play does not caricature or denigrate them. Nor does it show disrespect for the monarchy or question the role of secular authority, even if one agrees with Fassler, who hears in the music of Darius' decree when fooled by his counsellors the echo of "the 'hee-haw' of the ass" from the Feast of Fools.[63] Because Balthasar blasphemously misuses the vessels of God, he must die—a punishment that stands as a warning to all secular authority challenging God's representatives on earth. But when Darius' counsellors are envious and the law of the Medes and Persians is misused to attack Daniel, the right order is re-established by punishing the counsellors and declaring the precedence of God's law, not by overthrowing Darius or denying his laws.

At the play's conclusion, Daniel remains Darius' faithful counsellor, judge, and man of God. To borrow the terms of the post-colonial theory of Homi K. Bhabha, the play's representation of monarchy is a form of mimicry rather than mockery.[64] The play reflects the kind of "sly civility" that characterizes the discourse of the colonial subject. It suggests that although Daniel is, as exile, a subject to royal power, that power itself is actually subordinate to another, a power represented by Daniel. D. A. Bullough has commented that if there is any criticism implied by the *Ludus Danielis* it is "oblique" and it is "of bad counsellors rather than of arbitrary kingship."[65] In my view the play's criticism is far from oblique—the blasphemy of Balthasar and the envious actions of the royal counsellors are clearly punished. If the play is sometimes ambiguous regarding Darius, it is because Beauvais had an equivocal affiliation with the increasingly aggressive French crown. Whereas the *Ludus Danielis* explicitly condemns Balthasar and Darius' counsellors for their actions in the biblical past, it exhibits a sly civility toward the notion of monarchy in the present. The monarchy deserves respect—and the Queen even deserves praise. Nevertheless, royal authority is carefully placed within a hierarchy that subordinates secular to religious power. Most importantly, the play also implies a divine judgment upon any attempt to circumvent that hierarchy in the future.

The power of the religious—of Daniel and the bishop as men of God and wise judges—is made explicit through the performance of the biblical events. Here the "theatrical" locus, overlooked if we concentrate only on the text of the drama, is critical. For although the action of the play takes place in the land of exile—Babylon—the play's ceremonial activity and especially its metanarrative processions make clear that all is set within the spiritual sphere of Beauvais Cathedral and presented *sub specie aeternitatis*. Given the iconic connection between cathedral and Jerusalem, the action, though dramatically set in the Babylon of the biblical past, is nevertheless staged in the cathedral during the present. The play's sacred locus, in other words, suggests how the secular power of Babylon is enveloped by the power represented by Jerusalem. This power is visualized and the locus is made explicit when God's word—the famous handwriting on the wall—is literally written on the cathedral walls at the very moment when the sacred vessels are set before Balthasar: "Ecce sunt ante faciem tuam. *Interim apparebit dextra in conspectu Regis scribens in pariete:* Mane, Thechel, Phares" ("See, here they are before you. *Meanwhile a right hand appears before the*

King and writes on the wall: Mane, Teckel, Phares" [l. 60 and the following rubric]). It is at this moment that Daniel, the man of God and representative of the theocratic state of Jerusalem/Beauvais, is introduced to the action.

We cannot, of course, be certain of the play's staging in the Romanesque cathedral of Beauvais. Nevertheless, the threat of Babylon/Paris would have been suggested to the Beauvais audience if the actors playing Balthasar and his princes, moving in procession throughout the cathedral during the opening sequence, laid claim to its space as it summarized the biblical story (ll. 5–34). Secular hubris would then be made explicit if Balthasar actually ascended the bishop's cathedra when taking his throne: *"Tunc ascendat Rex in solium et Satrape ei applaudentes dicant:* Rex, in aeternum vive" (*"Then the king ascends his throne, and the Satraps, acclaiming him, say:* King, live forever" [l. 35]). The installation of the king in the bishop's throne would visualize the potential royal threat, underscored as the Satraps praise the blasphemous Balthasar as well as Nebuchadnezzar's victory over Jerusalem:

> Pater eius destruens Iudeorum templa,
> Magna fecit et hic regnat eius per exempla;
> Pater eius spoliavit regnum Iudeorum,
> Hic exaltat sua festa decore vasorum.
> (ll. 44–47)

> (When his father destroyed the temple of the Jews
> He did a great deed,
> And this king in his reign follows his father's example;
> His father looted the kingdom of the Jews;
> His son now embellishes his feasts
> With their splendid vessels.)

Even if a performance did not immediately coincide with one of the on-again, off-again crises between Beauvais and Paris, the play's emphasis on the Babylonian conquest of Jerusalem could easily bring to mind the possibility that Paris might well usurp the rights of Beauvais. Assuming a reasonably sophisticated audience sharing the bishop-count's theocratic claims, this jubilant sequence contrasting the joyful Babylon with the weeping Jerusalem (l. 56) would surely resonate with local significance. If as Fletcher Collins sug-

gests, furthermore, the objects used to represent Balthasar's desecration of the holy vessels of the temple were borrowed from the
cathedral treasury,[66] they would additionally equate temple and
cathedral, Jerusalem and Beauvais, Daniel and bishop, and, by implication, Babylon and Paris.

IV

If we heed Clifford Flanigan's call to understand medieval plays
as social practices "concerned with establishing a world view" within
particular communities, the *Ludus Danielis* is best understood not
only as commemorating the season of Christmas and as reforming
the Feast of Fools, but also as a communal action that in performance both reflects and helps propagate the ideology of Beauvais
throughout a crucial period in the history of the county-bishopric.
This approach examines the historicity of the play while recognizing
how it both represents salvation history and enacts concerns of import to contemporary history. This interpretation seeks to avoid
limiting the play to an "original meaning" defined by liturgical celebration or even by the intent to represent dramatically key moments
in salvation history as viewed through the lens of the four-fold exegetical method. Instead, it understands the play as a textualization
of history whose significance for the audience of Beauvais Cathedral
varies depending on the shifting circumstances of its complex relations with Paris. The play thus not only re-enacts but makes history
through each performance; it not only represents the "self-understanding" of Beauvais but "actually creates that self-understanding,"
to borrow again the words of Clifford Flanigan.[67]

The *Ludus Danielis*, in the reading I propose, is understood not
only as a biblical play serving a liturgical function, but also as a cultural practice supporting the theocratic ideology of Beauvais as it
defined itself in relation to the aggrandizing monarchy in Paris.
Whatever its "meaning" to its original audience, it must have continued to serve as a dramatic enactment of the unique circumstances
of a count-bishop whose combined secular and religious authority is
exemplified by Daniel, the wise judge and man of prayer, the counsellor of kings whose duty to God always remains paramount. Asso-
ciating Beauvais with Daniel, the temple, Jerusalem, and God, the

play in effect stages the boast made by Bishop Miles of Nanteuil to Blanche of Castille: "By Saint Peter everyone here should know that I have no *seigneur* in the world other than the Apostle, in whose protection I am: I do not answer to any other *seigneur*."[68] This challenge, enunciated around the time when the play was recorded in its present manuscript form, is both less elaborate and more blatant than the rich poetry and music of the *Ludus Danielis*. But it is a challenge which makes explicit the theocratic ideology of Beauvais that motivates the play's emphasis on the proper relation of religious and secular power. That it is voiced by the bishop is fitting, because it defiantly restates his ultimate loyalty to heavenly rather than to earthly power, to the apostle rather than to the king, to the papacy rather than to the monarchy. It also confirms his religious allegiance to Beauvais rather than to Paris, for the cathedral church of Beauvais is dedicated to St. Peter.[69] Just as the ambitious plans for its towering Gothic cathedral suggest that Beauvais planned a structure that would dwarf the earlier Gothic structures of Paris— both its cathedral of Notre-Dame and its royal abbey of St. Denis, the center of the textualization of royal ideology—so the *Ludus Danielis* represents in dramatic form the proud local traditions of Beauvais in contrast to the national claims of Paris and its increasingly powerful monarchy.

NOTES

[1] C. Clifford Flanigan, "Medieval Latin Music-Drama," in *The Theatre of Medieval Europe: New Research in Early Drama*, ed. Simon Eckehard (Cambridge: Cambridge Univ. Press, 1991), p. 37. Although I follow the edition published in the present volume, I have also consulted the edition in Karl Young, *The Drama of the Medieval Church* (Oxford: Clarendon Press, 1933), II, 290–301. The play is cited by line number in Young's edition. The translations are those published in the present volume unless otherwise noted. I dedicate this essay to the memory of Clifford Flanigan, whose research and innovative approaches to liturgical drama have had a profound and continuing effect on his many friends and admirers.

[2] Margot Fassler, "The Feast of Fools and *Danielis Ludus*: Popular Tradition in a Medieval Cathedral Play," in *Plainsong in the Age of Polyphony*, ed. Thomas Forrest Kelly, Cambridge Studies in Performance Practice, 2 (Cambridge: Cambridge Univ. Press, 1992), pp. 65–99. For a discussion of the poetic qualities of the work, see D'Arco Silvio Avalle, *Il teatro medieval e il ludus Danielis* (Turin: G. Giappichelli, 1984).

[3] Terry Eagleton, *Ideology: An Introduction* (London: Verso, 1991), p. 19, discussing Louis Althusser's understanding of ideology. Eagleton's introduction, "What Is Ideology?" (pp. 1–31), is both witty and helpful. My view of ideology is also influenced by Karl Mannheim, *Ideology and Utopia*, trans. Louis Wirth and Edward Shils (New York: Harcourt Brace, 1936).

[4] I am borrowing these issues from the "reader-response" theory of Stanley Fish; see his "Normal Circumstances, . . . and Other Special Cases," in *Is There a Text in This Class? The Authority of Interpretive Communities* (Cambridge: Harvard Univ. Press, 1980), pp. 268–92.

[5] C. Clifford Flanigan, "Comparative Literature and the Study of Medieval Drama," *Yearbook of Comparative and General Literature*, 35 (1986), 95–96.

[6] A facsimile of the play as it appears in the unique manuscript, British Library MS. Egerton 2615, fols. 95–108, appears in the present volume. For comment on the manuscript, see Gilbert Reaney, ed., *Manuscripts of Polyphonic Music, 11th–Early 14th Century*, International Inventory of Musical Sources, B IV, Vol. 1 (Munich: G. Henle, 1966), pp. 501–05, who states that "the codex was written during the pontificate of Gregory IX (1227–41) and probably before the marriage of Louis IX with Margaret of Provence (1234), in other words near the time when the cathedral foundation stone [for the present structure] was laid at Beauvais . . ." (p. 501). For a study of the manuscript, see Wulf Arlt, *Ein Festoffizium des Mittelalters aus Beauvais in seiner liturgischen und musikalischen Bedeutung* (Cologne: Volk, 1970), 2 vols.; for dating see pp. 29–30. For the Gothic rebuilding of Beauvais Cathedral, see Stephen Murray, *Beauvais Cathedral: Architecture of Transcendence* (Princeton: Princeton Univ. Press, 1989).

[7] John Baldwin, "Masters at Paris from 1179 to 1215: A Social Perspective," in *Renaissance and Renewal in the Twelfth Century*, ed. Robert L. Benson and Giles Constable (Cambridge: Harvard Univ. Press, 1982), p. 140.

[8] On the developing "religion of monarchy" in France, see Joseph R. Strayer, "France: The Holy Land, the Chosen People, and the Most Christian King," in *Medieval Statecraft and the Perspectives of History: Essays by Joseph R. Strayer* (Princeton: Princeton Univ. Press, 1971), pp. 300–14. My reading of the *Ludus Danielis* as an ideological response to the growing hegemony of Paris is akin to Gabrielle Spiegel's view that the rise of French vernacular prose history during this period was an aristocratic response to an increasingly powerful royal ideology ("Social Change and Literary Language: The Textualization of the Past in Thirteenth-Century Old French Historiography," *Journal of Medieval and Renaissance Studies*, 17 [1987], 129–48).

[9] See Jean Dunbabin, *France in the Making, 843–1180* (Oxford: Oxford Univ. Press, 1985), p. 256. The phrase "Rege regum et rege Francorum" is from the greeting of Epistola 187, in Suger, *Epistolae, Patrologia Latina* [henceforth *PL*], CLXXXVI, 1435–36.

[10] See especially John Baldwin, *The Government of Philip Augustus: Foundations of French Royal Power in the Middle Ages* (Berkeley and Los Angeles: Univ. of California Press, 1986). For an excellent study of the influence of royal ideology on manuscript illuminations during a later period of French history, see Anne D. Hedeman, *The Royal Image: Illustrations of the Grandes Chroniques de France, 1274–1422* (Berkeley and Los Angeles: Univ. of California Press, 1991).

[11] On the two genres of Daniel, see John J. Collins, *Daniel: A Commentary on the Book of Daniel* (Minneapolis: Fortress, 1993), pp. 38–61. For a helpful survey of the role of Daniel in literary texts, see the entry by Lawrence T. Martin in *A Dictionary of Biblical Tradition in*

English Literature, ed. David Lyle Jeffrey (Grand Rapids: Eerdmans, 1992), pp. 177–80.

[12] All biblical translations are from the Douay-Rheims translation of the Vulgate, rev. by Bishop Richard Challoner (1899; rpt. Rockford, Ill.: Tan Books, 1989).

[13] On Nebuchadnezzar's humbling in the fields, see Penelope B. R. Doob, *Nebuchadnezzar's Children: Conventions of Madness in Middle English Literature* (New Haven: Yale Univ. Press, 1974), pp. 54–94. Doob cites and translates Richard of St. Victor, *De eruditione hominis interioris*: "Nebuchadnezzar serves as an example that, whenever and however he pleases, God can humble those who walk in pride" (*PL*, CXCVI, 1348).

[14] Bernard of Clairvaux, *Lenten Sermons on the Psalm "He Who dwells,"* 17, in *Sermons on Conversion*, trans. Bernard Saïd, Cistercian Fathers Ser., 25 (Kalamazoo: Cistercian Publications, 1981), p. 257.

[15] The standard edition is *Commentarium Danielem*, Corpus Christianorum, 75A (Turnhout: Brepols, 1964), pp. 914–44. All translations are from *Jerome's Commentary on Daniel*, trans. Gleason L. Archer, Jr. (Grand Rapids: Baker Book House, 1958); for a study, see Jay Braverman, *Jerome's Commentary on Daniel: A Study of Comparative Jewish and Christian Interpretations of the Hebrew Bible*, The Catholic Biblical Quarterly Monograph Series, 7 (Washington, D.C.: Catholic Biblical Association, 1978). One significant twelfth-century commentary on Daniel that departs in interesting ways from Jerome is the "In Danielem Prophetam commentariorum" of Rupert of Deutz, included in his *De sancta Trinitate et operibus eius* [1112–16], ed. Hrabanus Haacke, Corpus Christianorum, Continuatio Mediaevalis, 23 (Turnhout: Brepols, 1972), pp. 1738–81. On Rupert, see John H. Van Engen, *Rupert of Deutz* (Berkeley and Los Angeles: Univ. of California Press, 1983).

[16] *Jerome's Commentary*, trans. Archer, p. 26.

[17] Commenting on *Dan.* 6.11, Jerome states: "From this passage we learn that we are not to expose ourselves rashly to danger, but so far as it lies in our power, we are to avoid the plots of our enemies. And so in Daniel's case, he did not contravene the king's authority in a public square or out in the street, but rather in a private place, in order that he might not neglect the commands of the one true God Almighty" (ibid., p. 66).

[18] Shakespeare, *Merchant of Venice* IV.i.223. Jerome does discuss Susanna and the Elders, following Origen's exegesis, but dismisses the stories of Bel and the Dragon. Genevra Kornbluth, "The Susanna Crystal of Lothar II: Chastity, the Church, and Royal Justice," *Gesta*, 31 (1992), 27, notes that early medieval exegesis interpreted the story of Susanna in three ways: (1) Susanna as a type of Ecclesia, (2) Susanna as a model of chastity, and (3) the judgment of Daniel as an example of just judgment. The references in the *Ludus Danielis* clearly follow the emphasis on just judgment evident in the third interpretive approach.

[19] According to de Lubac, *Exégèse Médiévale: Les Quatre sens de l'écriture*, Pt. 1, Vol. II (Paris: Aubier, 1964), 571–74, Daniel formed a trinity of Old Testament types that included Noah (ecclesiastics governing the church), Daniel (monastics or contemplatives), and Job (secular clergy or laymen). On Daniel as celibate see Augustine's *Enarrationes in Psalmos*, ed. D. Eligius Dekkers and Iohannes Fraipont, Corpus Christianorum, 40 (Turnhout: Brepols, 1956), p. 1929 (CXXXII.5). In the fifth book of the *Hypognosticon* of Lawrence of Durham (c.1100–54), a verse epic on salvation history based on the traditional six ages, Daniel represents hope in the traditional triad of faith (Abraham), hope, and charity (Christ). See A. G. Rigg, *A History*

of Anglo-Latin Literature, 1066–1422 (Cambridge: Cambridge Univ. Press, 1992), pp. 54–57.

[20] See Lawrence T. Martin, *Somniale Danielis: An Edition of a Medieval Latin Dream Interpretation Handbook* (Frankfurt: Peter Lang, 1981).

[21] Commenting on *Dan.* 6.4, Rupert states: "Danihel, cuius hoc ipsum nomen interpretatur *iudicium Dei*, typum hoc loco praefert Christi Filii Dei, cuius nimirum est iudicium Dei, quia Pater illi omne iudicium dedit" ("Daniel, whose name itself is interpreted *judgment of God*, here represents a type of Christ the Son of God, who without doubt is the judgment of God, because the Father gives all judgment to him" [*De sancta Trinitate*, p. 1752 [XXXII.11]). Unless otherwise noted, all translations from the Latin are mine. For Daniel as *iudicium Dei* see also Isidore of Seville, *In libros Veteris ac Novi testamenti proemia*, PL, LXXXIII, 169; and Rabanus Maurus, *De Universo*, PL, CXI, 67. To Rupert, Daniel is also a type of Christ in the false accusations that he suffers before Darius which foreshadow the trial of Christ before Pilate, and through Daniel's condemnation to the lions' den, which signifies Christ's descent into Hell (see *De sancta Trinitate*, pp. 1752–53 [XXXII.11]).

[22] Jerome established the basic interpretation, identifying the third empire as "that of the Macedonians" and the fourth as "the Roman Empire, which now occupies the entire world" (*Jerome's Commentary*, trans. Archer, p. 75). M.-D. Chenu, "Theology and the New Awareness of History," *Nature, Man, and Society in the Twelfth Century: Essays on New Theological Perspectives in the Latin West*, trans. and ed. Jerome Taylor and Lester K. Little (Chicago: Univ. of Chicago Press, 1968), p. 179, notes that Otto of Freising based his "imperial theology" on this standard interpretation of Daniel's four empires.

[23] *Jerome's Commentary*, trans. Archer, p. 77. This approach is evident not only in Jerome's commentary but also in the earliest patristic commentary on *Daniel* by Hippolytus (d. 235). Even for the later scholastics, Jerome's commentaries on *Daniel* and the *Apocalypse* and Augustine's *City of God* were the standard authorities for investigating the complexities of the Last Days. For example, Peter Damian states in *De novissimis et Antichristo* 2 (PL, CXLV, 838): "Quod itaque de die iudicii quaeris et Antichristo, lege librum beati Augustini De civitate Dei, et Expositionem sancti Hieronymi in Danielem prophetam, Apocalypsim quoque cum commentariis suis" ("Therefore if you want to know about the day of judgment and Antichrist, read the book of Saint Augustine *On the City of God*, and the *Exposition of Saint Jerome on the Prophet Daniel*, as well as the *Apocalypse* with his commentary"). On Antichrist, see Richard K. Emmerson, *Antichrist in the Middle Ages: A Study of Medieval Apocalypticism, Art, and Literature* (Seattle: Univ. of Washington Press, 1981).

[24] See *The Towneley Plays*, ed. Martin Stevens and A. C. Cawley, EETS, s.s. 13–14 (Oxford: Oxford Univ. Press, 1994), I, 71; *The N-Town Play*, ed. Stephen Spector, EETS, s.s 11–12 (Oxford: Oxford Univ. Press, 1991), I, 67; and *The Chester Mystery Cycle*, ed. R. M. Lumiansky and David Mills, EETS, s.s. 3, 9 (Oxford: Oxford Univ. Press, 1974–86), I, 400–402, 409.

[25] Cited by de Lubac, *Exégèse Médiévale*, Pt. 2, II, 249.

[26] Augustine notes that Daniel actually "specified the time when Christ was destined to come and to suffer, by giving the number of years that were to intervene" (*City of God*, trans. Henry Bettenson, ed. David Knowles (Baltimore: Penguin, 1972), p. 806 (XVIII.24). Jerome devotes a lengthy detailed historical explanation to this prophecy and cites several authorities but does not decide between them: "I realize that this question has been argued over in various ways by men of greatest learning, and that each of them has expressed his views according

to the capacity of his own genius. And so, because it is unsafe to pass judgment upon the opinions of the great teachers of the Church and to set one above another, I shall simply repeat the view of each, and leave it to the reader's judgment as to whose explanation ought to be followed" (*Jerome's Commentary*, trans. Archer, p. 95).

[27] Young, *The Drama of the Medieval Church*, II, 125–32, edits the sermon as it appears in a late twelfth-century lectionary from Arles, where it functions as the sixth *lectio* for Matins of Christmas. A similar role for Daniel is evident in other twelfth-century versions, for example that of Paris, Bibliothèque Nationale Lat. 1139, where Daniel appears between Jeremiah and Habakkuk to give his prophecy (Young, *The Drama of the Medieval Church*, II, 140). The sermon is now usually attributed to Quodvultdeus; see R. Braun, ed., *Opera Quodvultdeo Carthaginiensi episcopo tributa*, Corpus Christianorum, 60 (Turnhout: Brepols, 1976), pp. 225–58.

[28] See, for example, Marius Sepet, *Les Prophètes du Christ: Étude sur les origines du théatre au Moyen Age* (Paris: Didier, 1878), esp. pp. 49–61; Karl Young, "Ordo prophetarum," *Transactions of the Wisconsin Academy of Sciences, Arts, and Letters*, 20 (1922), 1–82; and Theo Stemmler, *Liturgische Feiern und geistliche Spiele: Studien zu Erscheinungsformen des Dramatischen im Mittelalter* (Tübingen: Max Niemeyer, 1970), pp. 107–11.

[29] On the relationship between the *Ludus Danielis* and the Daniel play composed by Hilarius (twelfth century; Paris, Bibl. Nat. Lat. 11331, ed. Young, *The Drama of the Medieval Church*, II, 276–86), see Young, who thinks either Beauvais borrowed from Hilarius or that both used a common source (ibid., II, 304). Oscar Cargill, *Drama and Liturgy* (1930; rpt. New York: Octagon, 1969), argued that Hilarius "unquestionably influenced" the Beauvais play (pp. 44–45), a view shared by Grace Frank, *The Medieval French Drama* (Oxford: Clarendon Press, 1954), p. 54. But Avalle, *Il teatro medieval,* p. 165, notes that the play includes a much wider range of poetic forms than does the Hilarius. Fassler, arguing against a direct relationship between the two plays, notes that "Although their plots and characterizations are similar, their texts are markedly different. In fact they are two independent attempts to accomplish the same end—allowing for popular elements of the Feast of Fools to be present through dramatizing a particular Old Testament story" ("The Feast of Fools and *Danielis Ludus*," p. 87). Both the Hilarius and the Beauvais *Daniel* are edited by Walther Bulst and M. L. Bulst-Thiele, *Notentext zu Hilarii Aurelianensis Versus et ludi, Epistolae, Ludus Danielis Belouacensis*, Mittellateinische Studien und Texte, 16 (Leiden: Brill, 1989), pp. 48–59 and 99–113.

[30] Jerome Taylor, "Prophetic 'Play' and Symbolist 'Plot' in the Beauvais *Daniel*," *Comparative Drama*, 11 (1977), 191–208, esp. 197–98. Fassler, "The Feast of Fools and *Ludus Danielis*," notes that Eastern-rite churches celebrate the feast of Daniel on 17 December (p. 71, n. 19).

[31] The thirteenth-century Laon *Ordo prophetarum*, for example, identifies him as "Daniel: adolescens, veste splendida indutus" ("Daniel: a youth, dressed splendidly" [Young, *The Drama of the Medieval Church*, II, 145]).

[32] See Taylor, "Prophetic 'Play' and Symbolist 'Plot'," p. 199; on the manuscript, see n. 6, above. Arlt, *Festoffizium*, I, 26, shows that the *Ludus Danielis* and the Circumcision Office were recorded by the same scribe. Commenting on this manuscript, Flanigan states that "Even a superficial glance at this liturgy, which includes many processions, hymns, sequences, tropes and tropes of tropes, with texts drawn from both biblical and classical sources, will put to rest the often repeated claim that the music-drama was a relatively rare 'paraliturgical' addition to a fixed and authorised liturgy. Rich and elaborate as the *Daniel* is, it is no more so than the liturgical celebration in which it was embedded" ("Medieval Latin Music-Drama," p. 37).

[33] This is a good example of how liturgical drama, according to Cynthia Bourgeault, "suddenly leaps 'out of character' into festival celebration" ("Liturgical Dramaturgy," *Comparative Drama*, 17 [1983], 124–40).

[34] Young, *The Drama of the Medieval Church*, II, 130.

[35] For the *Play of Adam*, see for convenience *Medieval Drama*, ed. David Bevington (Boston: Houghton Mifflin, 1975), pp. 78–121. The Nebuchadnezzar scene is on p. 121; see the rubric following l. 930 and ll. 931–44. For the Rouen *Ordo processionis asinorum secundum Rothomagensem usum*, see Young, *The Drama of the Medieval Church*, II, 154–65, esp. 164–65; see also John Wesley Harris, *Medieval Theatre in Context: An Introduction* (New York: Routledge, 1992), p. 40.

[36] For Babylon's symbolic role in the last days, see *Apocalypse,* chaps. 17–18. On Babylon as "ciuitas diaboli, ciuitas confusionis" ("city of the devil, city of confusion"), see Rupert of Deutz, *De sancta Trinitate*, p. 1750 (XXXII.9).

[37] It is worth remembering that the pseudo-Augustinian sermon and the Laon *Ordo* make clear that their prophecies apply to both the first and second advents of Christ. The sermon, for example, concludes with the Doomsday prophecy of the Sibyl—which is based on the prophetic verses in Augustine's *City of God* XVIII.23—and then notes that "Hec de Christi Nativitate, Passione, et Resurrectione atque secundo eius Adventu ita dicta sunt . . ." ("This is said concerning the Nativity, Passion, and Resurrection of Christ as well as his second Advent" [Young, *The Drama of the Medieval Church*, II, 131]).

[38] Rupert (*De sancta Trinitate*, p. 1751), for example, links the punishment of Belshazzar with the destruction of Babylon in *Apoc.* 18.2-3.

[39] Richard Axton, *European Drama of the Early Middle Ages* (Pittsburgh: Univ. of Pittsburgh Press, 1975), compares Daniel's release from the lions' den to the Harrowing of Hell and notes that it "was seen as foreshadowing Christ's resurrection from the tomb and the pit of hell" (p. 85). Although Axton cites no medieval source for this insight, the typological interpretation of Rupert of Deutz in *De sancta Trinitate* XXXII.11 noted above (see n. 21) supports this interpretation.

[40] For a visual representation of this scene, see the picture cycle cited by Fassler, "The Feast of Fools and *Danielis Ludus*," p. 84, fig. 4.2, from the Munich Psalter (Munich, Bayerische Staatsbibliothek MS. Clm. 835). The lower right scene on fol. 107ʳ represents Daniel, as if rising into heaven, lifted up by the angel; next to him a counsellor falls headlong into a lion's mouth and into the lions' den, there to join a cohort already being devoured by another lion. Visually this separation is reminiscent of Last Judgment scenes and may allude to both hell mouth and the traditional symbolism of left and right. It seems to me an iconographic image worth preserving when staging the play.

[41] Margot Fassler, "Representations of Time in *Ordo representacionis Ade*," in *Contexts: Style and Values in Medieval Art and Literature*, ed. Daniel Poirion and Nancy Freeman Regalado, *Yale French Studies*, special issue (1991), pp. 98, 100.

[42] See ll. 191–94, which conclude the praise of the Queen: "Nos quibus occasio ludendi/ hac die conceditur sollempni/ Demus huic preconia devoti,/ veniant et concinent remoti." Bevington translates these lines as follows: "Let us to whom the occasion of performing this play/ is

granted on this festive day/ Devotedly render praise to her,/ And let those from afar also come and join in song" (*Medieval Drama*, p. 145).

[43] Fassler, "The Feast of Fools and the *Danielis Ludus*," p. 66.

[44] Rainer Warning, "On the Alterity of Medieval Religious Drama," *New Literary History*, 10 (1979), 266.

[45] Young dates the play c.1140, a date repeated by Axton (*European Drama of the Early Middle Ages*, p. 77); this very early date seems driven by the desire to connect the *Ludus Danielis* to the Daniel play composed by Hilarius (see Young, *Drama*, II, 290, n. 4, and II, 303). William Tydeman, *The Theatre in the Middle Ages: Western European Stage Conditions, c. 800–1576* (Cambridge: Cambridge Univ. Press, 1978), states that the play was "composed by students of the choir-school at Beauvais for Christmas performance, c. 1180" (p. 58), but gives no basis for this later date. Frank (*The Medieval French Drama*, p. 56) dates the play to the middle of the twelfth century; Bevington does not date the play but simply notes that it is "the best known of twelfth-century dramas" (*Medieval Drama*, p. 137). Marcia J. Epstein's entry on the play in the *Dictionary of the Middle Ages* (New York: Scribner's, 1987), IX, 705–06, dates the play to the early thirteenth century. The late date (c.1230), most likely based on the date of the manuscript, is given by John Stevens, *Words and Music in the Middle Ages: Song, Narrative, Dance and Drama, 1050–1350* (Cambridge: Cambridge Univ. Press, 1986), p. 312. Although Fassler does not propose a date for the play, her emphasis on its association with the reformed Feast of Fools suggests a late twelfth- or early thirteenth-century date: "There is evidence that such reformers were at work at Beauvais in the late twelfth and early thirteenth centuries, and that the Circumcision Office and the Daniel play are somehow the results of this reform" ("The Feast of Fools and the *Danielis Ludus*," p. 82). For problems in determining provenance and dating of liturgical manuscripts, see Andrew Hughes, "Liturgical Drama: Falling Between the Disciplines," in *Theatre of Medieval Europe*, ed. Simon, pp. 44–46.

[46] The praise is from the chronicle of Helinand, a student of Ralph of Beauvais; see *PL*, CCXI, 1035. For Ralph, see R. W. Hunt, "Studies in Priscian in the Twelfth Century II: The School of Ralph of Beauvais," in *The History of Grammar in the Middle Ages: Collected Papers*, ed. G. L. Bursill-Hall (Amsterdam: John Benjamins, 1980), pp. 39–94. Hunt (p. 50) estimates that Ralph was in Beauvais by 1140, reached the height of his fame, c.1160–80, and was an old man in 1182–85.

[47] Murray, *Beauvais Cathedral*, p. 27; Murray's discussion of the political situation in Beauvais preceding the decision to rebuild the cathedral (pp. 27–49) is particularly helpful. He notes that in the early thirteeth century, Beauvais was the second city in the royal domain of France (p. 47).

[48] Elizabeth M. Hallam, *Capetian France, 987–1328* (London: Longman, 1980), p. 207.

[49] For the rights of the bishop of Beauvais, see Olivier Guyotjeannin, *Episcopus et Comus: affirmation et déclin de la seigneurie épiscopale au nord du royaume de France (Beauvais-Noyon, Xᵉ-début XIIIᵉ siècle)*, Memoires et documents publiés par la Société de l'École des Chartes, 30 (Geneva: Droz, 1987), pp. 3–31.

[50] On the relations between Philip I and Beauvais, see Hallam, *Capetian France*, p. 106.

[51] Quoted and translated by Murray, *Beauvais Cathedral*, p. 34.

[52] See Ch. Petit-Dutaillis, *The Feudal Monarchy in France and England from the Tenth to the Thirteenth Century*, trans. E. D. Hunt (London: Routledge and Kegan Paul, 1936), pp. 264–65.

[53] See Susan Reynolds, *Kingdoms and Communities in Western Europe, 900–1300* (Oxford: Clarendon Press, 1984), p. 176. See also Achille Luchaire, *Les Communes Françaises a l'époque des Capétiens directs* (Paris: Hachette, 1890), p. 239. For opposition to the communes as a contemporary form of "Babylon," see the sermon of Jacques de Vitri, quoted by Luchaire, pp. 242–44.

[54] Hallam, *Capetian France*, p. 237. Hallam notes that the bishop died shortly thereafter on his way to Rome.

[55] Bevington, ed., *Medieval Drama*, p. 145, n. to ll. 187–88.

[56] *Historia Pontificalis*, ed. and trans. Marjorie Chibnall, *Memoirs of the Papal Court* (New York: Nelson, 1956), pp. 69–70 (XXXV; italics mine). See also Suger's letter to Beauvais cited above (n. 9), *PL*, CLXXXVI, 1435–37. The French historian Olivier Guyotjeannin, whose *Episcopus et Comus* is the most detailed study of the rights and roles of the bishop-counts, has noted that the dispute between the two brothers was as much about family matters as about episcopal politics (p. 127). But in twelfth-century France, especially given the knotty relations between county-bishopric and monarchy, family matters often became episcopal and royal politics.

[57] Jerome states that "Josephus says she was Belshazzar's grandmother, whereas Origen says she was his mother. She therefore knew about previous events of which the king was ignorant" (*Jerome's Commentary*, trans. Archer, p. 58). Jerome also refutes Porphyry's identification of the queen as Belshazzar's wife.

[58] A lost manuscript described by Pierre Louvet, *Histoire et antiquitez du pais de Beauvais* (Beauvais, 1635), II, 200–302, contained a Feast of the Circumcision from Beauvais that referred to Louis VII and Adele. See Arlt, *Festoffizium*, p. 30; and Fassler, "The Feast of Fools and *Danielis Ludus*," pp. 82-83.

[59] The Hilarius *Daniel* does praise the Queen (ll. 156–75) but without alluding to Solomon's praise in *Proverbs* 31 (see Young, *The Drama of the Medieval Church*, II, 281).

[60] Bevington, for example, notes that the language of *Proverbs* "suggests that the 'spoils' are children" (*Medieval Drama*, p. 145, note to l. 186). The biblical verse states: "The heart of her husband trusteth in her, and he shall have no need of spoils" (*Prov.* 31.11).

[61] See Hedeman, *The Royal Image*, pp. 20–21, fig. 7; the miniature is from Paris, Bibliothèque Sainte-Geneviève MS. 782, fol. 280^r.

[62] Quoted by Jacques Le Goff, *Intellectuals in the Middle Ages*, trans. Teresa Lavender Fagan (Oxford: Blackwell, 1993), p. 21.

[63] Fassler, "The Feast of Fools and *Danielis Ludus*," p. 91. Making much of the "braying motive" at this point in the play, Fassler notes that "The Babylonians in their wickedness have become donkeys and fools," but she concedes that "Daniel the Prophet exposes the fools and, in so much as is possible in Old Testament time, saves the leader of the kingdom from his own

folly" (ibid., p. 92). She also notes that, unlike the Hilarius *Daniel*, the Beauvais play does not portray Darius as "iratus" (ibid., p. 91).

[64] See Homi K. Bhabha, "Of Mimicry and Man: The Ambivalence of Colonial Discourse," *The Location of Culture* (London: Routledge, 1994), pp. 85–92, esp. 86; see also the chapter, "Sly Civility," pp. 93–101.

[65] D. A. Bullough, "Games People Played: Drama and Ritual as Propaganda in Medieval Europe," *Transactions of the Royal Historical Society*, 5th ser., 24 (1974), 112.

[66] Fletcher Collins, Jr., *The Production of Medieval Church Music-Drama* (Charlottesville: Univ. Press of Virginia, 1972), p. 253. See ibid., pp. 242-55, for Collins' discussion regarding the staging of the *Ludus Danielis*.

[67] C. Clifford Flanigan, "Liminality, Carnival, and Social Structure: The Case of Late Medieval Biblical Drama," in *Victor Turner and the Construction of Cultural Criticism: Between Literature and Anthropology*, ed. Kathleen M. Ashley (Bloomington: Indiana Univ. Press, 1990), p. 48. Flanigan is here discussing Victor Turner's notion of ritual. My approach is also influenced by the New Historicist emphasis on "the historicity of texts and the textuality of history," as discussed by Louis A. Montrose, "Professing the Renaissance: The Poetics and Politics of Culture," in *The New Historicism*, ed. H. Aram Veeser (New York: Routledge, 1989), p. 20.

[68] Quoted by Murray, *Beauvais Cathedral*, p. 49.

[69] This is a point worth stressing, since it suggests how the divine and local are fused in the cathedral and its authority. Fassler mistakenly identifies Beauvais Cathedral as dedicated to St. Stephen ("The Feast of Fools and *Danielis Ludus*," p. 85).

The Play of Daniel
in Modern Performance

Fletcher Collins, Jr.

Consideration of modern performances of the Beauvais *Play of Daniel* seems worthwhile if only because it was the first of the medieval music-dramas to be revived, and further it has been so successful with audiences over the years that it has had more productions and has been given more performances than any other of the repertory. Yet the material of the play is atypical for the repertory, which elsewhere focuses substantially on New Testament narrative and the Christian saint's life. *The Play of Daniel* nevertheless has become the signature piece for medieval liturgical theater. To locate a medieval music-drama for someone unfamiliar with the genre, one has only to mention *The Play of Daniel* for instant recognition.

Because Noah Greenberg's production of the *Daniel* by his New York Pro Musica[1] in 1958 was the first modern staging, the circumstances and quality of that production merit detailed attention. Greenberg had already attracted critical approval of his Pro Musica concerts of early music, mainly of the Renaissance and pre-Bach periods, and he felt he could risk pulling one of the full-scale medieval music-dramas from Coussemaker's *Drames liturgiques du moyen âge*, published in 1860 as the first modern musical anthology of liturgical dramas. From conversation with Gustave Reese in 1963, I learned that he as mentor encouraged Greenberg to choose the *Daniel* as a colorful drama that had a useful connection with the Christmas season and that existed in a clear early thirteenth-century music manuscript, British Library Egerton MS. 2615. Greenberg then sought out Father Rembert Weakland, a musicologist familiar with medieval notation. Few persons then had attempted the transcription of a music-drama, though a generation earlier Pierre Aubry and Jean Beck had made transcriptions of troubadour-trouvère songs, and Weakland was aware that their melodic style was similar to that of the dramas of the same period. While he transcribed most of the *Daniel* items in conventional triple rhythm (3/4 and 6/8), he apparently offered five items in duple (2/2 and 4/4), four of these of considerable length. The fact that in the performing edition, published by Oxford University Press in 1959, these four are spaced at regular intervals (pages 21–25, 45–50, 61–67, 83–85) suggests that either Weakland or Greenberg (as editor) wished for some relief from the strictly medieval triple rhythm through some alternation with duple. In observance of another basic principle, Weakland respected the accented syllables of the verses as invariably requiring the first (i.e., strong) beat of the measure, though occasionally he settled for false accents, most notably on page 70 where there are eight such uncharacteristic solutions—or was this the result of Greenberg's direction of the singers and his editing?

There were other difficulties with this first attempt at a performing edition of the *Daniel*. As I wrote more than two decades ago, "Greenberg's production . . . was hedged and protected by so many additions and modifications that the performance might be most accurately described as skillful adaptation of the original playscript."[2] These additions were: (1) ten passages of pastiche English verse by the well-known poet W. H. Auden, intrusive narrations spoken by an invented Monk, and amounting to sixty-two percent of the total vocal lines of the adaptation; (2) a large number of instrumental items, non-existent in the Beauvais text as it appears in Egerton MS. 2615, and constituting nearly as many measures of the total adaptation as those of the source's unaccompanied singing; (3) the unnecessary invention of Balthasar's Prince, a role the manuscript properly assigns to the Satraps; and (4) the irrational move of the Queen's conductus from the chorus of the Satraps to the Queen herself.

Greenberg chose Lincoln Kirstein, who was prominent but had no experience with medieval theater, as the producer, "taking charge of direction, staging, and costumes"; Kirstein said that he "wanted to do something that would be worthy of The Cloisters."[3] Nikos Psacharopoulos, with a reputation as a professional stage director, served in that capacity for the *Daniel* for this production. Presiding over his production was of course Noah Greenberg, who had no theater experience and was concentrating his efforts on the musical score, which he expanded, edited, and conducted from the monophonic score that had been commissioned from Weakland. Greenberg told me in 1962 that when he was presented by Weakland with several possible transcriptions of an item, he had no trouble choosing "whichever was the most beautiful." Those were the good old days when the ugly head of "authenticity" had only been slightly raised, though Greenberg acknowledged "the responsibility to present both an historically 'accurate' version as well as living performances."[4]

The first performances of *The Play of Daniel* were in January 1958 in the Romanesque Hall of The Cloisters, a superb museum overlooking the Hudson River in upper New York City. Greenberg had promoted and publicized his production extensively and in the right places. After opening night, the *New York Times* dean of drama critics, Brooks Atkinson, declared that the play was an "hour-long invocation to glory."[5] The "especially devised" costumes and the set were not quite at home in the twelfth-century surroundings, and this was so in spite of the advice of scholars, Margaret Freeman of The Cloisters and Meyer Schapiro of Columbia University. But at that triumphant moment this did not matter: the explosive energy of Greenberg's *Daniel* established it as the bellwether of the medieval music-drama revival.

Nor was the Beauvais play, originating and appropriate in the large spaces of the Beauvais Cathedral, entirely happy in the comparatively small Romanesque Hall. The following year Greenberg was able to move the production to the vast National Cathedral in Washington, D.C., where spectacular effects—e.g., the slow dim-out of the hugely winged Angel at the end of the play—were fully possible. Greenberg told me that he had to have two miles of electric cable laid down from outside the Cathedral to power the stage lighting. The *Daniel* played there at Christmastide for several years and also toured extensively in the United States and abroad.

A complete chronological history of these and other performances of the Greenberg *Daniel* is beyond the scope of the present account. Jerome Taylor quite accurately noted in 1977 that the edition, disk recording, and performances of the *Daniel* by the Pro Musica had "stimulated school groups, church groups, indeed academics in professional conclave, to attempt faithful reproduction of the play."[6] Margot Fassler similarly begins her essay on the *Daniel* with the statement that "it undoubtedly still appears in live performances more regularly and often than any other medieval drama with music."[7] Prior to 1982, when the semi-annual *Medieval Music-Drama News* began publication, there was no systematic effort to record, archivally and critically, the various productions of the *Daniel* and the other plays in the repertory.

Greenberg's *Daniel* not only motivated interest in the performance of medieval music-dramas but was also, according to Harry Haskell in his appraisal of the revival of early music, "the Pro Musica's most brilliant single achievement."[8] One can only speculate on what would have been the consequences if Greenberg had chosen another play from the repertory for his initial production. His second production, *The Play of Herod*—a conflation of the Fleury *Herod* and *Killing of the Innocents* plays—initially rode on the momentum of the *Daniel*. Greenberg's death in 1966 and the inevitable fading of the momentum also doomed *The Play of Herod*.

Scholarly studies of the nature, form, and development of the liturgical plays have centered on the Easter plays, from the tropes to the full-blown *Visitatio Sepulchri* such as the one included in the Fleury Playbook. The *Daniel*, fortunately or unfortunately, was surprisingly neglected in the scholarship for the 1965–75 period when we would instead expect interest to have risen.[9] And the neglect has continued. An obvious reason for less study of the *Daniel* is that its liturgical connections are not entirely within the same forensic area as those of the Easter plays. The *Daniel* is not even central to the Advent liturgy, though in the Middle Ages it was dominant in the parodic celebrations of the Feast of Fools, as revealed in Margot Fassler's exemplary essay.[10]

In an early departure from the Greenberg style, the Department of Music at the University of Leeds presented as a mid-day concert on 23 November 1972 a performance of the first half of the play in the University's mid-Victorian Emmanuel Church. The transcription was from W. L. Smoldon's original edition, later than Weakland's. The actors were students of Richard Rastall, who was the music director while Jane Oakshott served as dramatic director. Rastall recalls:

> We did not take too liturgical a view of the drama: that is, we costumed it in secular fashion and did not try to use liturgical gesture or movement (except in the broadest sense in the processions). But we were not anxious to follow the Greenberg style in New York. In the end we used no instruments at all: not even the organ, and not even in the processions. This was to force the

students to listen and carry the drama vocally rather than from any idealism or move toward "authenticity," although it happens I did not approve of Greenberg's introduction of minstrel instruments.[11]

At Christmas 1976 the Collegium Musicum (directed by Mary Anne Ballard) of the University of Pennsylvania presented the *Daniel* with Cynthia Bourgeault providing stage direction. This production was to see a total of sixteen performances in the Philadelphia area, with revivals in the same area in 1978 and 1980. The script and score were faithful to the Egerton Manuscript and to the relevant chapters of biblical narrative. Otherwise from the 1970's I have only a few records of producer, place, and date for *Daniel* performances in America. One is supplied in the article by Jerome Taylor which has been cited above: "the play was produced by the Collegium Musicum of the Southern Baptist Theological Seminary, Jay Wilkins, Director, at the Second Annual Medieval Conference sponsored jointly by the Seminary and the University of Louisville, February 15–16, 1974, in Louisville, Ky."[12] Another production is recorded in California. According to its director, D. Kern Holoman, the Early Music Ensemble of the University of California, Davis, played the *Daniel* "between December 1975 and February 1976 . . . at five campuses of the University of California and in churches and museums. It was jointly sponsored by the Departments of Music and Dramatic Art." Holoman noted, however, that they played "most often . . . in small theatres rather than churches."[13]

Abroad, however, the Clerkes of Oxenford brought the *Daniel* back to its place of origin in Beauvais in 1975, as reported by David Wulstan, who presumably was the director.[14] Further, the same issue of *Early Music* that had noticed Holoman's California production announced that "A Production of *The Play of Daniel* by David Munrow and the Early Music Consort of London will have its first performance at the 1976 Aldeburgh Festival."[15] This production was, of course, not to be. Christopher Hogwood wrote in the *Dictionary of National Biography* that Munrow "developed a strong feeling for the liturgical repertoire of the late medieval and Renaissance periods; shortly before he died he was planning a reformed consort to explore this territory."[16] We can only grieve for the loss of such a production of *Daniel* and of an early music leader comparable in influence to Noah Greenberg, who also had died far too young.

By the 1980's other early music ensembles seeking to produce the *Daniel* required lavish funding and facilities to mount the play in the Greenberg manner. Notable among them were the New York Ensemble for Early Music (founded in 1974) and Joel Cohen's Boston Camerata (founded in 1954). The New York group was led by Frederick Renz. Cohen, bringing the *Daniel* in November 1982 to the Medieval Court of the Metropolitan Museum of Art (not The Cloisters' Romanesque Hall), said, "It was our feeling that it would be no honor to the memory of that magnificent being [Greenberg] simply to revive his most famous production," and so proceeded to "rethink anew the great masterpiece of the past."[17]

In his transcription and production of the *Daniel*, Renz, at home in December 1982 in the huge choir of St. John the Divine in New York City, was less inclined to "rethink anew" and preferred to remove some of the "improvements and glitter" and to "carry out further notions of characterization and narrative focus," as his stage director, Paul Hildebrand, testified, having earlier with the Folger Consort attempted a *Daniel* (22 March 1982) in which belly dancers and a winking Chinese lion were featured. Renz and his Ensemble progressed to production at the Spoleto Festival in Italy (29 June–10 July 1983) in a small Spoleto church, and returned to New York for performances in the immensities of St. John the Divine.

Canadian productions of the *Daniel*, in Montreal and Toronto, appeared in late 1983 and early 1984. On 27 November the choir of Queen Mary Road Church, Montreal, with Carol Harris-Taylor as music director, performed the Collins transcription of the play, fully staged with the assistance of Steven Lecky and Karen Young. The *mise en scène* was in a Victorian Gothic church, with due attention to the obligatory processionals. Later this group participated in a different kind of performance of the same score at Bishop's University, Lennoxville, where the choir sang the script and actors effectively mimed the characters. The following 28–30 January and 4–6 February saw Timothy McGee's transcription performed in Toronto by the veteran Poculi Ludique Societas (PLS). It was an elaborate production, with a chorus of eleven from New York, seven undergraduate instrumentalists from the University of Toronto, and stage direction by David Parry.

Later that year the New York Ensemble for Early Music played at the other Spoleto Festival, in Charleston, South Carolina, at the Cathedral of St. John the Baptist. In 1985 the Early Music Ensemble again performed the *Daniel* at St. John the Divine and toured it to the University of Maryland at College Park (19 October) and Princeton (21 October). In the next year the Early Music Ensemble played in Iowa and Texas and also abroad in Sicily, Viterbo, Rieti, Rome, followed by performance at the Israel Festival in Jerusalem, where the troupe played in the open-air court of David's Citadel (29 May–4 June 1986). The same year they returned to Italy and played in Sicily, Citania, Palermo, Messina, and Rome. In 1987 the group played in Ilmajoki, Finland, within a two-thousand-seat circus tent (the temperature was 50 degrees F.). In the summer of 1988 the EEM took the *Daniel* to the Edinburgh Festival (20–25 August), to Cracow (29–30 August), and to venues in six southeastern states in the United States. After a year away from the play, they traveled with the *Daniel* to Hong Kong (12–14 February 1990), and then in the next year they played in Brisbane, Australia (20–25 May 1991), where the locally enlisted choral group was made up of the cathedral choir boys. Dramatic director for these performances, except for the Hong Kong production, was Paul Hildebrand.

The Boston Camerata's production style at the Metropolitan Museum in 1982 was much more influenced by the Pro Musica's flamboyant strategies, designed to overwhelm Broadway critics by innovative effects, gorgeous costuming, and medieval dance pieces, though Joel Cohen had only five instrumentalists on stage at a time. While Greenberg had invented a Monk and added Auden's narration, Cohen concocted a country-American preacher, in prose. Greenberg retained the great *Te Deum laudamus* as the finale, but Cohen substituted the nineteenth-century American shape-note hymn *Wondrous Love* and supplemented the Beauvais text with recitations from English literature and the Sephardic chant from the *Lamentations of Jeremiah.* These items were included, according to Cohen, "to draw us closer to the spiritual center of the Daniel drama." The vocal quality of Cohen's singers was more medieval, having been directed by Andrea von Ramm, the guest star playing Daniel as countertenor and tenor; the Pro Musica's Charles Bressler had been a more Wagnerian tenor. Andrew Porter in *The New Yorker* described the setting, the Medieval Court, as "unnuminous and concert-like," and would have preferred a church setting for "both the sound and the drama."[18]

Meanwhile, the Cathedral of St. John the Evangelist in Milwaukee presented *The Play of Daniel* on 11–15 December 1985 in the Pro Musica edition with program credits to the Most Reverend Rembert Weakland, now Archbishop of Milwaukee, who was also properly credited with the transcription for the Pro Musica edition. But not all of the rising confidence to follow the professionals into the realm of the *Daniel* was well placed. For example,

> The effort by the choir and soloists of the Park Place Baptist Church in Norfolk, Virginia, on December 18, 1983, was unseasoned, though somewhat making up in enthusiasm what it lacked in finish. Because of the lack of time in the singers' Christmas commitments, the music director chose to do without a stage director and permitted the performers to remain on book throughout. The result was of course more like an oratorio, yet costumed and blocked. Many of the *Daniel conductus* items require choreography and did not receive it. . . . To their credit the Park Place Baptists were saying, with a wry smile after the performance, that they hope to have their production of the *Daniel* ready by the next Christmas.[19]

In Europe the Grand Theater of Warsaw, Poland, was to open an elaborate and professional repertory production of *Ludus Danielis* from the Beauvais manuscript. Kenneth Nafziger of Eastern Mennonite College reported to me his enthusiasm for the performance that he saw and that he described as "one of the most exciting experiences of medieval theater." In the program notes the director, Robert Satanowski, described the mission of the players: "We believe that the present production enriches our sense of community with that bygone era. . . . It is so universal that even today one can present it to an audience."[20] At this time, in 1984, Poland was still subservient to the former Soviet Union, and audiences naturally identified themselves with Daniel as an impoverished political exile, "pauper et exulans." The theater atmosphere was similar to that of Anouilh's production of *Antigone* during the Nazi occupation of Paris forty years earlier.

In the American Midwest, the American Medieval Players presented the *Daniel* in my transcription in six Chicago-area churches on 4–6 and 11–13 April 1986 with Andrew Schultze directing. The play in this production was framed by and integrated into a *festa fatuorum*, a Feast of Fools. There was a donkey as well as the usual lions, and a modest amount of instrumental accompaniment and interscenic bridges. In the Cathedral Church of Christ the King in Kalamazoo, the *Daniel*, as transcribed and edited by Audrey Davidson, was performed by the Society for Old Music (founded in 1966 by Audrey Davidson, a veteran of approximately a dozen liturgical dramas) and the Western Michigan University Collegium Musicum (Matthew Steel, director) on 2 December 1990. The dramatic director was Clifford Davidson for this production, which utilized the spacious modern cathedral with its abundant theatrical areas for the conductus processions and the *sedes*.

The architectural settings of the more than twenty productions of the *Daniel* were much more often ecclesiastical than secular. As indicated above, the original modern production of Noah Greenberg was set in a museum gallery space that, according to its curator,

> provided an ideal setting for this 12th century play, with its stone walls and vaulting, its 12th century French doorway, and above this arched portal the colorful 12th century Spanish fresco of the Virgin and Child whose coming Daniel prophesied. Another fresco to the right of the audience depicted a fierce and salmon-pink lion, and at the left a sculptured lion from the Cathedral of Zamora provided a kind of canopy for the throne of the king.[21]

Greenberg also furnished The Cloisters with a number of architectural set-piece constructions, inspired mainly by eleventh-century Catalan manuscript illuminations. These additions contrived the throne, the lions' den, and Daniel's house. It would be another fifteen years before additional research would make available a more probable style of twelfth-century sets.[22] Greenberg's intention was pragmatic: to use the materials at hand, chiefly art and artifacts from The Cloisters, and the period instruments of the Pro Musica consort. In these respects the style for this pace-setting production encouraged the adventurous.

Most producers of the *Daniel*, as a matter of economy, have not attempted to use a museum setting but have worked with existing church architecture, usually buildings inspired by medieval designs: Gothic Revival cathedrals, Victorian Gothic churches, replications like the National Cathedral in Washington to which Greenberg came after The Cloisters. The chancels of the churches were favorable playing spaces because they frequently followed the medieval practice of elevating their floors by a number of steps, thereby improving the sightlines for an audience in rows of pews (a fourteenth-century innovation) down a long nave. The difficulty with sightlines is more pronounced for a play than for a concert, and often leads groups who perform in cathedrals to build extensive platforms. Greenberg himself opted for platforms at the National Cathedral.

Adequate lighting has been another problem in ecclesiastical spaces. Greenberg's two miles of cable have been noted above; the difficulty there and elsewhere was compounded by the small capacity of the church electric system. Architects naturally did not anticipate a theatrical demand and only slightly improved on the taper-and-torch conditions of the medieval.

When producers for various reasons preferred to stage *Daniel* in the well-wired secular space of an auditorium, they found certain trade-offs: the modern stage lighting of an auditorium-style theater, with raked seating for good audience sightlines, was countered by the unsympathetic architecture. For example, the *Daniel* production by the Folger Consort at Baird Hall of the Smithsonian Institution was forced to use the raked aisles through the five-hundred-seat auditorium for the eleven conductus processions, the proscenium opening not being wide enough to permit the usual medieval premise of *sedes* at left and right or a large *platea* area in the middle for transitional scenes and some processions.

Unfortunately, many churches have inadequate playing space in chancels that are pre-empted by choir stalls, riser platforms, built-in lecterns, pulpits, fonts, and other trappings. Thus the preponderance of church-related *Daniel* productions has not been located in ideal spaces. The chief advantage of a church has been that its religious atmosphere got the performance off in the right way—a condition remarkably different from that of the secular picture-stage of the auditorium or the bland outdoor platform. In addition, the latter often presents serious acoustical difficulties.

Other venues for *Daniel* performances have been encountered by groups on tour, notably the Early Music Ensemble in concert-style platforms at the Edinburgh Festival, in the previously-mentioned two-thousand-seat circus tent in Finland or the ruins of David's Citadel in Jerusalem, in oriental Hong Kong, and in Brisbane, Australia. The EEM has adapted the staging of the *Daniel* to this variety of spaces and has demonstrated what good troupers have always accepted—i.e., that the only minimum requirement is "three boards and a passion."

These "three boards" have recently been in the form of the

Cathedral of Christ the King, Kalamazoo, and the Church of the Transfiguration (The Little Church Around the Corner) in New York City, on 5 and 8 May 1994, the "passion" being provided by the Schola Cantorum "Quem Quaeritis" of the Netherlands with A. Marcel J. Zijlstra as music director and staging by Dunbar H. Ogden. Melody S. Owens' review of this production emphasized its success "in providing a glimpse of the 'feel' of medieval performance practice."[23] The ten-man Schola sang *a cappella* in high-collared monastic robes. There were no instruments, save the human voice, and no scenes and machines. They carried candles in procession. The lions' den was a side chapel, the lions' presence only in the voices within the chapel. The writing on the wall was mimed.

In contrast with the Schola production was the most recent performance of the *Daniel* prior to the publication of this book. This performance was another Toronto presentation, by the Toronto Consort, assisted by the PLS, in Trinity-St. Paul's United Church on 3 November 1995. David Klausner was stage director, David Fallis the musical director and transcriber of the music. Fallis' program notes provide information about the intent of the performance and present his impression that the use of musical instruments in the play was an expression of rebellion. While such a view is unlikely in the light of Fassler's research, he is quite correct in seeing the *Daniel* as a less liturgical piece than, for example, the *Visitatio Sepulchri* though "still animated by the spirit of liturgical celebration." In this context he sees the *Daniel* presenting problems in its relationship to the Feast of Fools and its expanded use of secular melodies. The melodies that are involved, however, are likely to be less uniquely secular than the program notes suggest.

One may conclude that all productions of the *Daniel* in our day—indeed, all productions of the liturgical music-dramas—fall somewhere along a spectrum between the opulent Greenberg and EEM performances at one extreme and the simple Dutch performance at the other.

NOTES

[1] Noah Greenberg christened his group the New York Pro Musica Antiqua (in imitation of Safford Cape's Pro Musica Antiqua of Brussels), but soon dropped the "Antiqua."

[2] Fletcher Collins, Jr., *The Production of Medieval Church Music-Drama* (Charlottesville: Univ. Press of Virginia, 1972), p. 245.

[3] Record liner notes, p. 12 (Decca DL 9402).

[4] *The Play of Daniel*, ed. "for modern performance" by Noah Greenberg (New York: Oxford Univ. Press, 1959), p. ix.

[5] Quoted by Margaret B. Freeman; record liner notes, p. 12 (Decca DL 9402).

[6] Jerome Taylor, "Prophetic 'Play' and Symbolist 'Plot' in the Beauvais *Daniel*," *Comparative Drama*, 11 (1977), 192.

[7] Margot Fassler, "The Feast of Fools and *Danielis Ludus*: Popular Tradition in a Medieval Cathedral Play," in *Plainsong in the Age of Polyphony*, ed. Thomas Forrest Kelly (Cambridge: Cambridge Univ. Press, 1992), p. 65.

[8] Harry Haskell, *The Early Music Revival: A History* (London: Thames and Hudson, 1988), p. 110.

[9] See C. Clifford Flanigan, "The Liturgical Drama and Its Tradition: A Review of Scholarship 1965–75," *Research Opportunities in Renaissance Drama*, 18 (1975), 81–102, and 19 (1976), 109–36.

[10] Fassler, "The Feast of Fools and *Danielis Ludus*," pp. 65–99.

[11] Personal communication from Richard Rastall (5 Oct. 1994).

[12] Taylor, "Prophetic 'Play' and Symbolist 'Plot'," p. 206.

[13] *Early Music*, 9 (1976), 162–63.

[14] *The Play of Daniel: A Medieval Liturgical Drama*, transcribed by W. L. Smoldon, rev. ed. by David Wulstan (Plainsong and Mediaeval Music Society, 1976), p. v.

[15] *Early Music*, 9 (1976), 163.

[16] Christopher Hogwood, "David Munrow," *Dictionary of National Biography*, Suppl. (1971–80), p. 619.

[17] Quoted in "Five Golden Rings," *Medieval Music-Drama News*, 2 (1983), 1.

[18] Quoted in Andrew Porter's review of the Boston Camerata's production, in *The New Yorker*, 29 Nov. 1982, pp. 170–71.

[19] "Two Daniels," *Medieval Music-Drama News*, 3 (1984), 2.

[20] Translated by Christopher Collins for *Medieval Music-Drama News*, 4 (1985), 8.

[21] Freeman, in record liner notes, p. 12 (DL 9402).

[22] See my *Production of Medieval Church Music-Drama, passim.*

[23] *The Early Drama, Art, and Music Review,* 17 (1994), 57.

Music in the Beauvais *Ludus Danielis*

Audrey Ekdahl Davidson

The *Ludus Danielis* from Beauvais Cathedral has been a remarkably popular work ever since its modern revival by Noah Greenberg and the New York Pro Musica in 1958; the principal reasons for its popularity are clearly its melodic inventiveness and the coherence achieved by its musical structure. The play, preserved in the unique manuscript, British Library Egerton MS. 2615, fols. 95ʳ–108ʳ, and known to scholars since it was first edited by Edmond de Coussemaker in 1860, was, according to the statement in the first item of the play, devised and presumably presented by youths at the Cathedral of Beauvais.[1] Associated with the Christmas octave, it apparently was, as Margot Fassler has argued, part of a reform movement determined upon supplanting the lewd frivolity and even sacrilege of the Feast of Fools when secular clergy and minor orders traditionally engaged in role reversal and other outlandish behavior— e.g., drinking wine before the church door, bringing an ass into the cathedral, and censing the altar with pudding and sausage.[2] These rites were celebrated as a culmination of the ceremonies belonging to deacons (Feast of St. Stephen, on 26 December), to priests (Feast of the Apostle St. John, on 27 December), to acolytes and boys of the cathedral (Feast of the Innocents, on 28 December), and to subdeacons (Feast of the Circumcision, ordinarily on 1 January).[3] The *Ludus Danielis* quite plausibly can be seen as part of the design to bring some order out of the chaotic yearly celebrations of youths and minor clerical orders, in particular of the subdeacons.

As a play written by and for the boys and minor clergy of Beauvais, the drama is a blending of two stories regarding the prophet Daniel. The first concerns the downfall of King Balthasar (Belshazzar) because of his and his father's desecration of the sacred vessels taken from the temple at Jerusalem; coincidentally, these reflect the liturgical vessels normally in the care of the subdeacons.[4] The

second focuses, during the time of King Darius, on Daniel's incar-
ceration in the lion's den for refusing to relinquish the worship of
his own God. The biblical sources for these episodes are *Daniel*,
Chapters 5–6, and the apocryphal *Bel and the Dragon*, the latter
supplying the Habakkuk incident. These actions are framed by a
series of processions which, in their one note-one syllable melodic
form and their nearly hypnotic repetitions, drive the action forward
and contribute to the power that Jerome Taylor noted when he said
that even amateur groups are able "to evoke a moving religious experience"[5] through the play. The dramatic effect emphasizes the prophetic element in the drama, for, appropriately with regard to the
Christmas season, the events are linked to the prophecy of Christ's
birth.[6]

The notation, characteristic for late twelfth- and early thirteenth-
century Northern France, is marked by the canted *punctum*, a
rhomboid shape.[7] It is written on a staff of four red lines, and, while
clearly showing individual pitches, the notation leaves room for
more than a single interpretation with regard to rhythmic values;
however, as John Stevens observes, a number of "melodies with
their strongly accentual Latin verse texts seem to invite the metrical
interpretation that most editors give them."[8] Medieval theorists such
as Guido of Arezzo provide corroboration for the metrical interpretation of plainchant and, by extension, of plainchant in liturgical
drama; Guido says: "I speak of chants as metrical because we often
sing in such a way that we appear almost to scan verses by feet, as
happens when we sing actual meters."[9]

The processions which frame the action are related to the liturgical conductus, the purpose in the liturgy being that of bringing the
reader of the lesson to the lectern.[10] In *Ludus Danielis* suitable processions, usually labeled *conductus*, are introduced for each character as he or she proceeds to his or her destination. The strongly accented *prosa, Astra tenenti cunctipotenti* (ll. 5–34),[11] though not
marked in the rubric as a conductus, nevertheless functions similarly for the entrance of Balthasar's princes; it also serves to identify
the Beauvais singers as "virilis et puerilis." The piece consists of
nine appearances of the A melody; the hypnotic repetition coupled
with the driving, strongly accented rhythm combine to emphasize
the ideas of the text: the heavenly might and power of the Creator of

the firmament, King Balthasar's earthly and temporal power, and Daniel's sagacity, which will prevail beyond that of Balthasar's reign. The Latin verse of this item is seen by John Stevens as being particularly apt for a metrical musical rendering[12] (see Example 1).

EXAMPLE 1

The Satraps' processional song, *Iubilemus Regi nostro*, accompanying the bringing of the purloined vessels to the King (ll. 40–59) is a liturgical item which also appears in the Laon Epiphany office as *Jubilemus cordis voce*.[13] The song as it appears in the *Ludus Danielis* opens with the following melodic progression:

EXAMPLE 2

This melody, which is syllabic, proceeds stepwise with the addition of two short leaps of a major third. The strong resemblance of the piece to *Orientis partibus* (*Prose of the Ass*, from the Beauvais Circumcision Office also contained in Egerton MS. 2615, fols. 1^r–2^r and 43^r–44^v) has been observed by Fassler, who comments that "[t]he use of this melody both within a special Office designed for the sub-deacons at Laon and in the Beauvais Daniel play points to the asso-ciation the piece had for this particular tripudium and strengthens the argument that the Babylonians in *Ludus Danielis* were meant to be recognized as subdeacons in disguise."[14] Thus there is additional evidence for the subdeacons as the ones impersonating those charac-ters in the play who brought out the ill-gotten vessels in order to drink from them in an improper and possibly even blasphemous celebration. For the audience, the echoes of the *Song of the Ass* also would have established a secular, even satiric context for *Iubilemus Regi nostro*; coupled with the accents of the poetry which drive the piece into a metrical rhythmic rendition, the piece achieves a kind of youthful vitality. Conversely, Taylor has perceived this item as be-ing "jingly" and even silly.[15]

The conductus *Cum doctorum et magorum* that accompanies the Queen's entrance and passage to the King (ll. 75–98) is marked by a beautiful melody which first falls and then rises. The melody fits the description of the Queen as "prudent" or "sagacious" (*prudens*) and as having power (*cum potentia*). Her wisdom is more fully displayed in the next item when she suggests that the prophet Daniel be con-sulted to interpret the words written on the wall; nevertheless, the conductus that brings her in foreshadows her active role in the play. The melody is marked by melismas strategically placed (four notes on the syllable "-rum" of *doctorum* and four notes on the syllable "ma-" of *magorum*), notes which ripple downward gracefully (Example 3).

EXAMPLE 3

si - o.

Interestingly, the first four notes of the beautiful melody which signifies the Queen—the g g–e f motif—are borrowed from her conductus and are used for Daniel's procession at *Hic verus Dei famulus* (ll. 122–26);[16] Daniel then sings the motif as, setting out to meet the King, he describes his exiled condition in a macaronic statement: "Pauper et exulans envois al Roi par vos" (l. 127). The use of the vernacular French for "I go with you to the King" marks Daniel as a man of the people. Ultimately, the motif from the Queen's conductus will be echoed six times as Daniel processes. The individuality of the melody and its ability to distinguish character may be blunted, but the qualities of dignity and wisdom, possessed by both the Queen and Daniel, are underlined.

Daniel's speech to the King—*Rex tua nolo munera* (ll. 147–76)—although not strictly accompanying a procession, still has the one syllable–one note pattern which is characteristic of the conductus. It is as if Daniel were pacing as he speaks to the King. He refuses the immense gifts offered by the King, and then identifies Balthasar's culpability when he lists the crimes of his father Nebuchadnezzar; concluding the catalogue of sins, he finally reveals the meaning of the mysterious message on the wall. The musical setting includes numerous appearances of a pervasive melody with its transpositions and variants, all obviously related. These repetitions build up suspense for the elucidation of the riddle which appears in the last three appearances of the melody.

Daniel's message having been heard, the Queen takes her leave. Perhaps because her entrance music has been used by Daniel and the princes, a different conductus, *Solvitur in libro Salomonis*, is used for her exit (ll. 181–94). The piece, again praising her wisdom, has fourteen lines of verse paired in an *ouvert-clos* manner, as Mathias Bielitz has noted.[17] The rhythm of the text falls into a triple meter which should be taken at a dignified but not solemn pace (see Example 4). Any seeming satisfaction that the text conveys can only be ironic, since the message as deciphered by Daniel holds no happy results in store for either the Queen or the King.

EXAMPLE 4

Sol - vi - tur in li - bro Sa - lo - mo - nis Di - gna laus et con - gru - a ma - tro - nis. Pre - ci - um est e - ius si quam for - tis Pro - cul et de fi - ni - bus re - mo - tis.

Following the departure of the Queen, the conductus *Regis vasa referentes*, accompanying the act of bringing the vessels before Daniel (ll. 195–215), praises the prophet in a repeated refrain: "Gaudeamus, laudes sibi debitas referamus." Its poetic structure, shaping the musical form, seems related to the litany as transformed into a secular strophic *laisse* with refrain. The strophes in this song are irregular, with new material inserted at the second and fourth strophes. Here the poetic meter can be fitted to a strongly duple musical rhythm, and the song moves along with vigor. The refrain is strengthened when the notes setting the text "Gaudeamus" are lengthened to emphasize their importance. The jubilant text, steady rhythm, and words of praise and rejoicing are, in the light of Balthasar's fate, ironic.

The arrival of the triumphant King Darius and Balthasar's subsequent expulsion also could occasion another procession, although not strictly labeled such. In *Ecce Rex Darius* (ll. 216–45), the mentioning of musical instruments, citharas and organs, does not necessarily indicate that these would have been used in a liturgical context, though they are not by nature to be seen as decadent in

themselves. However, in connection with the entrance of the Persian
king and his princes, who are said to be dancing (*tripudia*), these instruments could well have been played in such a way as to be signs
of the depravity of the Medes and Persians.

Daniel, having been recommended to the new King, is led to
Darius with *Congaudentes celebremus*, which has a melody that
moves along in what must be triple metered rhythm (ll. 270–84).
The text, celebrating both the prophet Daniel and the birth of
Christ, credits Daniel with foretelling the new Christian era; in his
wisdom and faithfulness to God, Daniel is revealed as a type of
Christ.[18] The structure of the song is comprised of six repeated A
sections (with variants in higher and lower ranges), three B sections
at the center, and then six A sections with variants to close—an
ABA or arch form.[19]

EXAMPLE 5

This joyous moment is, of course, not to last. The envious counsellors advise Darius to create a law prohibiting the worship of any

gods other than the King Darius; Daniel, praying to the God of
Judea, is the one deliberately caught in their trap. Daniel is led to
the lions' den; realizing his plight, the prophet laments: "Heu, heu,
heu" (ll. 342–49). The repetition of the words on a single note in this
instance is particularly affecting.

The depiction of the Angel's protection of Daniel in the lion's den
is not marked by any framing conductus, nor can the music for another Angel's message to Habakkuk—*Abacuc, tu senex pie*—be construed as rhythmically measured (ll. 358–61). Habakkuk's rejoinder
Novit Dei cognitio quod Babylonem nescio (ll. 362–65) is a straight-
forward melody, for the most part syllabic and chant-like in the logic
of its intervals, moving up and down the Dorian mode in seconds
and thirds. The Angel's action of seizing Habakkuk by the hair and
forcing him to go to the lions' den would seem to be a comic detail,
but there is nothing inherently humorous in the music. Habakkuk's
words to Daniel in the item *Surge, frater, ut cibum capias* (ll. 366–
69) are set to mostly syllabic music with several four-note melismas
interspersed: the melismas occur on *Sur-* of *Surge*, on *gra-* of *gratias*,
and on *qui*. A kind of word-painting appears on the rising notes
setting the syllable *Sur-*.

The movement of the characters near the close of the play is accompanied by less elaborate music, not to be construed as full-scale
processions. King Darius goes to the den and laments, then finds
Daniel alive. The envious counsellors are led to the den, and their
words are remarkable for their recognition of their responsibility for
their fate. King Darius rejoices, Daniel prophesies, and the Angel
announces the birth of Christ in Bethlehem with a hymn, *Nuntium
vobis fero de supernis* (ll. 389–92).[20] After the long, elaborate processions in the earlier part of the play, the relative calm of the end-
ing is almost surprising. The *Te Deum*, suggesting performance at
Matins in Beauvais Cathedral, concludes what remains today a most
satisfying drama. Then as now one comes away from a performance
of the play quite aware of the overarching pattern of the music. The
music both accompanies and carries the action in the drama from
moment to moment, from unrest to climactic tension to this finale in
rest and revelation.

NOTES

[1] See Henry Copley Greene, "The Song of the Ass," *Speculum*, 6 (1931), 535n, for the observation that British Library, Egerton MS. 2615 was probably written "during the pontificate of Gregory IX (1217–41) and before the marriage of Louis IX to Marguerite of Provence in 1234." This conjecture is based on the fact that the *Officium* included in the same manuscript gives prayers for Pope Gregory and King Louis, but there are no prayers for Queen Marguerite. For the contents of the manuscript, see *Catalogue of Additions to the Manuscripts in the British Museum in the Years 1882–1887*, pp. 336–37, and Augustus Hughes-Hughes, *Catalogue of Manuscript Music in the British Museum* (London: British Museum, 1906), I, 242, 253; see also Richard Emmerson, "Divine Judgment and Local Ideology in the Beauvais *Ludus Danielis*," n. 6, in the present volume, for further references.

[2] Margot Fassler, "The Feast of Fools and *Danielis Ludus*: Popular Tradition in a Medieval Cathedral Play," in *Plainsong in the Age of Polyphony*, ed. Thomas Forrest Kelly (Cambridge: Cambridge Univ. Press, 1992), pp. 72, 87–88, 97; cf. E. K. Chambers, *The Mediaeval Stage* (London: Oxford Univ. Press, 1903) I, 287, who cites a mock procession from Beauvais in the thirteenth century.

[3] Fassler, "The Feast of Fools," p. 69.

[4] Ibid., p. 88.

[5] See Jerome Taylor, "Prophetic 'Play' and Symbolist 'Plot' in the Beauvais *Daniel*," *Comparative Drama*, 11 (1977), 192.

[6] Ibid., p. 199.

[7] See John Stevens, "Medieval Drama," *New Grove Dictionary of Music and Musicians*, ed. Stanley Sadie (London: Macmillan, 1980), XII, 31. The transcription of *Ludus Danielis* by A. Marcel J. Zijlstra in the present book gives a rhythmic setting to a number of the items in the play.

[8] Stevens, "Medieval Drama," p. 31. The regular rhythmic interpretation of the music in *Ludus Danielis* is given support by David Hiley in *Western Plainchant: A Handbook* (New York: Oxford University Press, 1993), p. 270, who comments. "In the first half of the piece nearly every entrance or exit of characters is accompanied by vigorously rhythmic conductus." See also Hiley's discussion of medieval rhythmic theories in "Notation, III, I: Western, plainchant," *New Grove*, XII, 351. Hiley cites, among others, Aurelian of Réôme (d. 850) and Guido of Arezzo (c. 1030), whose works point toward the metrical rendering of chant and the music of liturgical drama.

[9] Guido of Arezzo, *Micrologus*, trans. Warren Babb, in *Hucbald, Guido, and John on Music: Three Medieval Treatises*, ed. Claude V. Palisca (New Haven: Yale Univ. Press, 1978), p. 72. It seems probable that the medieval composers of liturgical music set the Latin metrical verse to music governed by the rhythmic modes. Both Fletcher Collins, Jr., and William L. Smoldon have argued for the use of the rhythmic modes in transcribing liturgical drama. Collins remarks, "The metric units of nearly all verse in the plays are either trochaic, iambic, or dactyllic, which have musical analogues in what are called rhythmic modes" (*Medieval Church Music-Dramas: A Repertory of Complete Plays* [Charlottesville: Univ. Press of Virginia,

1976], p. xi). Smoldon presents a similar position: "As the centuries passed, the admission into Church music-drama libretti of more and more rhyming Latin poetry of regular scansion made it obvious that settings of such lyrical compositions, though written in plainchant notation, were more than likely to have been interpreted . . . through some kind of use of the 'rhythmic modes,' or at least, in something other than 'free rhythm'" (*The Music of the Medieval Church Dramas*, ed. Cynthia Bourgeault [London: Oxford Univ. Press, 1980], p. 36n).

[10] John Stevens, *Words and Music in the Middle Ages: Song, Narrative, Dance, and Drama, 1050–1350* (Cambridge: Cambridge Univ. Press, 1986), p. 56.

[11] Line numbers refer to the edition of Karl Young, *The Drama of the Medieval Church* (Oxford: Clarendon Press, 1933), II, 290–301, though I have throughout cited the musical items and quoted directly from the manuscript. I have adopted Zijlstra's musical transcription in the present volume for my musical examples.

[12] Stevens, "Medieval Drama," p. 31.

[13] Hiley, *Western Chant*, p. 270.

[14] Fassler, "The Feast of Fools," p. 89.

[15] Taylor, "Prophetic 'Play' and Symbolist 'Plot'," p. 203.

[16] Hiley notes that *Hic verus Dei famulus* "has the same melody as the Benedicamus song *Postquam celorum dominus* in Paris 1139" (*Western Chant*, p. 270).

[17] My discussion of forms in *Solvitur in libro Salomonis*, *Regis vasa referentes*, and *Congaudentes celebremus* is indebted to Mathias Bielitz' analysis in *Hilarii Aurelianensis: Versus et Ludi: Epistolae: Ludus Danielis Belouacensis*, ed. Walther Bulst and M. L. Bulst-Thiele (Leiden: E.J. Brill, 1989).

[18] Taylor, "Prophetic 'Play' and Symbolist 'Plot'," p. 205.

[19] Bielitz, No. 34, in *Hilarii Aurelianensis*, ed. Bulst and Bulst-Thiele.

[20] See Susan Rankin, "Liturgical Drama," in *The Early Middle Ages*, ed. Richard Crocker and David Hiley, New Oxford History of Music, 2 (Oxford: Oxford Univ. Press, 1990), p. 350.

The Play of Daniel
(*Ludus Danielis*)

Transcribed by A. Marcel J. Zijlstra

Editorial Notes
on the Transcription

The present transcription of *The Play of Daniel* was initially prepared for a performance in May 1994 at the twenty-ninth International Congress on Medieval Studies at Kalamazoo. For this occasion I made a fresh transcription of the play from the manuscript, British Library, Egerton MS. 2615, and provided new interpretations of the rhythm.[1] Hence, the transcription should be regarded not only as an interpretation of a medieval source but also as a written report of a recent performance. This factor accounts for the mixing of notation, both rhythmical and with stemless noteheads. Whenever the chant has a strong, almost inevitable "drive" I have chosen a rhythmic transcription, while when the rhythm seems to be guided by the Latin word accents mainly rather than by a rigid meter I have adopted stemless noteheads. Sometimes also I have used the alternation of rigid meter and free rhythm for dramatic effect. For example, in the dialogue between King Darius and his envious entourage, the law-abiding counselors sing in strict 4/4 meter, and in answering them the King sings in a free rhythm, which establishes the effect of his reluctance and feelings of insecurity. It will also be noted that in

---

[1] The history of modern transcriptions of the play begins with Edmond de Coussemaker in 1860 (reprinted in an appendix to Walther Bulst and M. L. Bulst-Thiele, *Hilarii Aurelianensis Versus et ludi, Epistolae: Ludus Danielis Belouvacensis* [Leiden: Brill, 1989]). Karl Young, in *The Drama of the Medieval Church* (Oxford: Clarendon Press, 1933), II, 290–301, presented the first reliable text but did not include the music. The transcription of Rembert Weakland, as edited by Noah Greenberg and including instrumentation by E. A. Bowles (New York: Oxford Univ. Press, 1959), was the first practical performing edition, followed closely by the edition of William L. Smoldon (London: Oxford Univ. Press, 1960), whose transcription was in stemless notation. The transcription by Fletcher Collins, Jr. (*Medieval Church Music-Dramas* [Charlottesville: Univ. Press of Virginia, 1976], pp. 399–458), provides rhythmic notation and also is designed for practical performance. The present edition is the first to include both transcription and a facsimile of the folios in the manuscript containing the play.

Vir propheta Dei I have used a 5/4 meter. This seems awkward, as no irregular meters are known from medieval theory. However, as a result of experimentation during rehearsals, the singers felt that this was the only meter that fitted the text, and for this reason I chose to adopt it.

Quite clearly no single way of interpreting the music of the Beauvais *Daniel* can ever be determined to be the "authentic" manner of producing it. It will be axiomatic that anyone wishing to perform these melodies should try to *feel* the rhythm present in both texts and music and then to sing the words according to his musical skills.

A translation of the Latin text has been provided following the musical transcription.

Notes on the Musical Transcription:

Plicas are indicated with ♪ on top of the staff.
In some strophic songs not every couplet has exactly the same music:

> *Solvitur in libro Salomonis*, seventh couplet: de*v*oti has no *plica g–f*, but only g (as the first couplet).
> *Audite principes regalis*, third couplet: Baltha*sar* has only d, not e–d.
> *Decreverunt in tua curia*, first couplet: *De*creverunt has only c, the second stanza has a plica c-b.
> *Ecce venit*, first stanza: *san*ctorum has a single g, the plica g–f is in the second stanza.
> *Congaudentes*, eleventh couplet: ag*mine* ends with c–b b in the manuscript.

Textual Notes:

> *Regis vasa:* MS.: et cetera = ed.: Laudes sibi debitas referamus
> *Ecce rex Darius:* MS.: confirgit = ed.: confregit
> *Congaudentes:* MS.: flaflamine = ed.: flamine
> *Nunquid Dari:* MS.: muminibus = ed.: numinibus
> *Huius rei:* MS.: partronum = ed.:patronum

INCIPIT DANIELIS LUDUS

Ad ho - no - rem tu - i, Chri - ste, Da - ni - e - lis lu - dus i - ste.

in Bel - va - co est in - ven - tus. et in - ve - nit hunc iu-ven-tus.

Dum venerit Rex Balthasar, Principes sui cantabant ante eum hanc prosam:

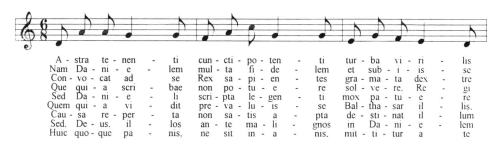

A - stra te - nen - ti cun - cti - po - ten - ti tur - ba vi - ri - lis
Nam Da - ni - e - lem mul - ta fi - de - lem et sub - i - is - se
Con - vo - cat ad se Rex sa - pi - en - tes gra - ma - ta dex - tre
Que qui - a scri - bae non po - tu - e - re sol - ve - re. Re - gi
Sed Da - ni - e - li scri - pta le - gen - ti mox pa - tu - e - re
Quem qui - a vi - dit pre - va - lu - is - se Bal - tha - sar il - lis.
Cau - sa re - per - ta non sa - tis a - pta de - sti - nat il - lum
Sed. De - us. il - los an - te ma - li - gnos in Da - ni - e - lem
Huic quo - que pa - nis, ne sit in - a - nis, mit - ti - tur a te

et pu - e - ri lis con - ti - o plau - dit.
at - que tu - lis - se fir - mi - ter au - dit.
qui si - bi di - cant e - nu - cle - an - tes:
i - li - co mu - ti con - ti - cu - e - re.
que pri - us il - lis clau - sa fu - e - re.
fer - tur in au - la pre - po - su - is - se.
o - re le - o - num di - la - ce - ran - dum.
tunc vo - lu - i - sti es - se be - ni - gnos.
pre - pe - te va - te pran - di - a dan - te.

91

Tunc ascendat Rex in solium et Satrape ei applaudentes dicant:

Rex, in e - ter - num vi - ve!

Et Rex apperiet os suum dicens:

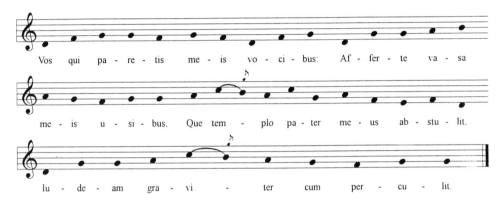

Vos qui pa - re - tis me - is vo - ci - bus: Af - fer - te va - sa

me - is u - si - bus. Que tem - plo pa - ter me - us ab - stu - lit.

Iu - de - am gra - vi - ter cum per - cu - lit.

Satrape vasa deferentes cantabunt hanc prosam ad laudem Regis:

Iu - bi - le - mus Re - gi no - stro ma - gno ac po -
Re - so - net io - cun - da tur - ba sol - lem - pni - bus

ten - ti. - Re - so - ne - mus lau - de di - gna
o - dis. Cy - tha - ri - zent, plau - dant ma - nus.

vo - ce com - pe - ten - ti. Pa - ter e - ius
mil - le so - nent mo - dis.

de - stru - ens Iu - de - o - rum tem - pla.

Ma - gna fe - cit, et hic re - gnat e - ius per e -

no - ris: Re - so - ne - mus o - mnes u - na

lau - di - bus so - no - ris. Ri - dens plau - dit

Ba - by - lon. Ihe - ru - sa - lem plo - rat.

Hec or - ba - tur, hec tri - um - phans Bal - tha - sar a -

do - rat. O - mnes er - go e - xul - te - mus

tan - te po - tes - ta - ti, Of - fe - ren - tes

re - gis va - sa su - e ma - ies - ta - ti.

Tunc Principes dicant:

Ec - ce sunt an - te fa - ci -

em tu - am.

Interim apparebit dextra in conspectu Regis scribens in pariete:

Mane, Thechel, Phares.

Quam videns Rex stupefactus clamabit:

Tunc adducentur magi, qui dicent Regi:

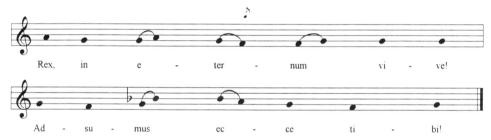

Et Rex:

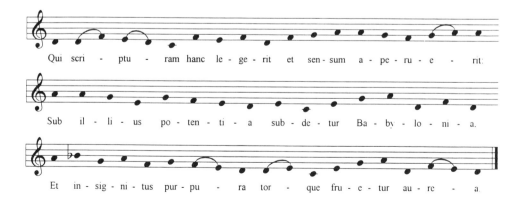

Illi vero nescientes persolvere, dicent Regi:

Ne-sci-mus per-sol-ve-re nec da-re con-si-li-um: Que sit su-per-scri-pti-o, nec ma-nus in-di-ti-um.

Conductus Regine venientis ad Regem:

Cum doc-to-rum   et ma- - go-rum om-nis ad- -sit con-ti- -
Ec-ce pru-dens, styr-pe clu-ens, di-ves cum po-ten-ti- -

o.   Se-cum vol- -vit ne-que sol-vit   que sit   ma-nus vi-
a: In ves-ti- -tu de-au-ra-to   con-iunx   ad-est re-

si - o.   Hec la-ten-tem   pro-met   va-tem per cu-
gi - a.

ius in-di-ci- -um: Rex de-scri- -bi su-um i-bi

no-ve- -rit e-xi-ti- -um.   Le-tis er-go   hec

vi- -ra-go co-mi-te- -tur plau-si- -bus: Cor-dis, o-

ris-que so-no-ris   per-so- -ne-tur vo-ci- -bus.

Tunc Regina veniens, adorabit Regem dicens:

Rex, in e - ter - num vi - ve!

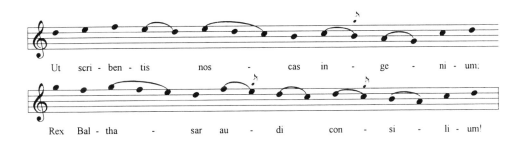

Ut scri - ben - tis nos - cas in - ge - ni - um:

Rex Bal - tha - sar au - di con - si - li - um!

Rex audiens hec versus Reginam vertet faciem suam. Et Regina dicat:

Cum lu - de - e cap - ti - vis po - pu - lis

Pro - phe - ti - e doc - tum o - ra - cu - lis

Da - ni - e - lem a su - a pa - tri - a

Ca - pti - va - vit pa - tris vic - to - ri - a.

Hic sub tu - o vi - vens im - pe - ri - o.

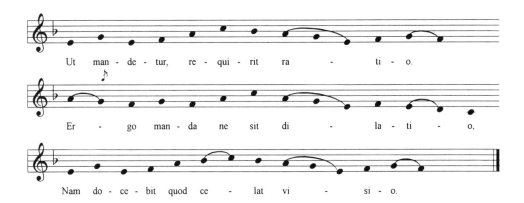

Ut man - de - tur, re - qui - rit ra - ti - o.

Er - go man - da ne sit di - la - ti - o,

Nam do - ce - bit quod ce - lat vi - si - o.

Tunc dicat Rex Principibus suis:

Vos Da - ni - e - lem que - ri - te; et in - ven - tum ad - du - ci - te.

Tunc principes invento Daniele, dicant ei:

Vir pro - phe - ta   De -   i,   Da - ni - el: Vien   al   Roi.   Ve -
Pa - vet et tur -   ba -   tur,   Da - ni - el: Vien   al   Roi.   Vel -
Te di - ta - bit   do -   nis,   Da - ni - el: Vien   al   Roi.   Si

ni   de - si - de - rat par - ler   a   toi.
let   quod nos la - tet sa - voir par   toi.
scri -   pta po - te - rit sa - voir par   toi.

Et Daniel eis:

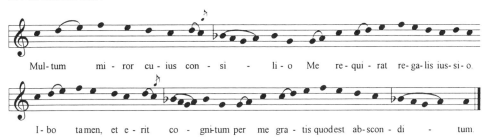

Mul-tum mi-ror cu-ius con-si - li-o Me re-qui-rat re-ga-lis ius-si-o.

I-bo ta-men, et e-rit co - gni-tum per me gra-tis quod est ab-scon-di - tum.

Conductus Danielis venientis ad Regem:

Hic ve - rus De - i fa - mu-lus, quem lau - dat o - mnis

po - pu-lus: Cu - ius fa - ma pru-den - ti-e est no - ta re - gis

cu - ri-e. Ce - stui man-da li Rois par nos! Pau-per et e-xu -

lans en - vois al Rois par vos. In iu - ven-tu - tis

glo - ri - a, ple-nus ce - les - ti gra - ti-a, Sa - tis ex-cel - lit

o - mni-bus vir-tu - te, vi - ta, mo - ri-bus; Ce - stui man-da li

Rois par nos! Pau - per et e-xu - lans en-vois al Roi par vos.

Hic est cu-ius au-xi-li-o sol-ve-tur il-la

vi - si - o, In qua scri - ben - te dex - te - ra mo - ta sunt Re - gis

vi - sce - ra; Ce - stui man - da li Rois par nos! Pau - per et e - xu -

lans en - vois al Roi par vos.

Veniens Daniel ante Regem, dicat ei:

Rex, in e - ter - num vi - ve!

Et Rex Danieli:

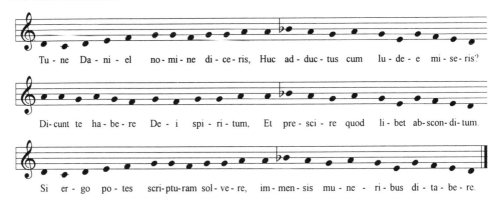

Tu - ne Da - ni - el no - mi - ne di - ce - ris, Huc ad - duc - tus cum Iu - de - e mi - se - ris?

Di - cunt te ha - be - re De - i spi - ri - tum, Et pre - sci - re quod li - bet ab - scon - di - tum.

Si er - go po - tes scrip-tu-ram sol - ve - re, im - men - sis mu - ne - ri - bus di - ta - be - re.

Et Daniel Regi:

Rex, tu - a no - lo mu - ne - ra; gra - tis sol - ve - tur

li - te - ra. Est au - tem hec so - lu - ti - o: in - stat ti - bi con -

fu - si - o. Pa - ter tu - us pre o - mni - bus, po - tens o - lim po -

ten - ti - bus, Tur - gens ni - mis su - per - bi - a, de - iec - tus est

a glo - ri - a. Nam cum De - o non am - bu - lans, sed

se - se de - um si - mu - lans: Va - sa tem - plo di - ri - pu - it, que

su - o u - su ha - bu - it. Sed post mul - tas in - sa - ni - as, tan -

dem per - dens di - vi - ti - as, For - ma nu - da - tus ho - mi - nis pa -

stum gu - sta - vit gra - mi - nis. Tu quo - que e - ius fi - li - us, non

i - pso mi - nus im - pi - us, Dum pa - tris ac - tus se - que - ris, va -

sis e - is - dem u - te - ris. Quod, qui - a De - o dis - pli - cet, in -

stat tem - pus quo vin - di - cet. Nam scri - ptu - re in - di - ci - um mi -

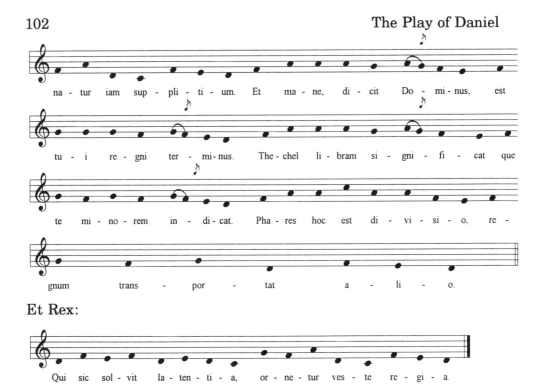

na - tur iam sup - pli - ti - um. Et ma - ne, di - cit Do - mi - nus, est

tu - i re - gni ter - mi - nus. The - chel li - bram si - gni - fi - cat que

te mi - no - rem in - di - cat. Pha - res hoc est di - vi - si - o, re -

gnum trans - por - tat a - li - o.

Et Rex:

Qui sic sol - vit la - ten - ti - a, or - ne - tur ves - te re - gi - a.

**Sedente Daniele iuxta Regem induto ornamentis regalibus, exclama-
bit Rex ad Principem militie:**

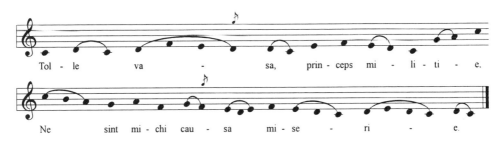

Tol - le va - sa, prin - ceps mi - li - ti - e.

Ne sint mi - chi cau - sa mi - se - ri - e.

**Tunc relicto palatio referrent vasa Satrape;
Et Regina discedet.**

Conductus Regine:

Sol - vi - tur in li - bro Sa - lo - mo - nis Di - gna laus et

con - gru - a ma - tro - nis.

Pre - ci - um est
Fi - dens est in
Mu - li - er hec
E - ius nam fa -
Nos qui - bus oc -
De - mus huic pre -

e - ius si quam for - tis
e - a cor ma - ri - tis
il - li com - pa - re - tur
cun - di - a ver - bo - rum
ca - si - o lu - den - di
co - ni - a de - vo - ti.

Pro - cul et de fi - ni - bus re -
Spo - li - is di - vi - ti - bus po -
Cu - ius rex sub - si - di - um me -
Ar - gu - it pru - den - ti - am doc -
hac di - e con - ce - di - tur sol -
ve - ni - ant et con - ci - nent re -

mo - tis.
ti - ti.
re - tur.
to - rum.
lem - pni,
mo - ti.

Conductus referentium vasa ante Danielem:

Re - gis va - sa re - fe - ren - tes, quem Iu - de - e tre - munt gen - tes.

Da - ni - e - li ap - plau - den - tes. Gau - de - a - mus.

Lau - des si - bi de - bi - tas re - fe - ra - mus!

Re - gis cla - dem pre - no - ta - vit, Cum scri - ptu - ram re - se - ra - vit.

Tes - tes re - os com - pro - ba - vit. et Su - san - nam li - be - ra - vit.

Gau - de - a - mus; Lau - des si - bi de - bi - tas,

re - fe - ra - mus! Ba - by - lon hunc e - xu - la - vit

Cum Iu - de - os cap - ti - va - vit. Bal - tha - sar quem ho - no - ra - vit.

Gau - de - a - mus; Lau - des si - bi de - bi - tas

re - fe - ra - mus. Est pro - phe - ta san - ctus De - i,

hunc ho - no - rant et Cal - de - i, Et gen - ti - les et Iu - de - i.

Er - go iu - bi - lan - tes e - i, Gau - de - a - mus;

Lau - des si - bi de - bi - tas, re - fe - ra - mus.

Statim apparebit Darius Rex cum Principibus suis, venientque ante
eum cythariste et Principes sui psallentes hec:

Ec - ce rex Da - ri - us ve - nit cum prin - ci - pi - bus no - bi - lis no - bi - li - bus.

E - ius et cu - ri - a re - so - nat le - ti - ti - a, ad - sunt et tri - pu - di - a.

Hic est mi - ran - dus, cun - ctis ve - ne - ran - dus. Il - li im - pe - ri - a sunt tri - bu - ta - ri - a; Re - gem ho - no - rant o - mnes et a - do - rant. Il - lum Ba - by - lo - ni - a me - tu - it et pa - tri - a. Cum ar - ma - to ag - mi - ne. ru - ens et cum tur - bi - ne. ster - nit co - hor - tes. con - fre - git et for - tes. Il - lum ho - nes - tas co - lit et no - bi - li - tas. Hic est Ba - by - lo - ni - us no - bi - lis rex Da - ri - us. Il - li cum tri - pu - di - o gau - de - at hec con - ti - o. Lau - det et cum gau - di - o E - ius fac - ta for - ti - a tam ad - mi - ra - bi - li - a. Si - mul o - mnes gra - tu - le - mur: re - so - nent et tym - pa - na; Cy - tha - ris - te tan - gant cor - das; mu - si - co - rum or - ga - na Re - so - nent ad e - ius pre - co - ni - a.

Antequam perveniat Rex ad solium suum duo precurrentes expellent Balthasar quasi interficientes eum. Tunc sedente Dario Rege in maiestate sua, Curia exclamabit:

Rex, in e - ter - num vi - ve!

Tunc duo flexis genibus secreto dicent Regi ut faciat accersiri
Danielem. Et Rex iubeat eum adduci. Illi autem aliis precipientes,
dicent hec:

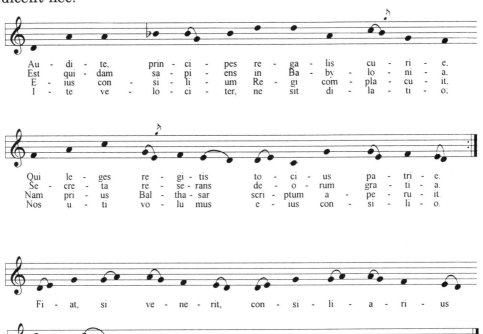

Au - di - te,   prin - ci - pes re - ga - lis   cu - ri - e.
Est qui - dam   sa - pi - ens in Ba - by - lo - ni - a.
E - ius con - si - li - um Re - gi com - pla - cu - it.
I - te ve - lo - ci - ter, ne sit di - la - ti - o:

Qui le - ges   re - gi - tis   to - ci - us   pa - tri - e.
Se - cre - ta re - se - rans   de - o - rum gra - ti - a.
Nam pri - us Bal - tha - sar scri - ptum a - pe - ru - it.
Nos u - ti vo - lu - mus e - ius con - si - li - o.

Fi - at, si ve - ne - rit, con - si - li - a - ri - us

Re - gis,   et fu - e - rit in re - gno ter - ci - us.

Legati invento Daniele, dicent hec ex parte Regis:

Ex re - ga - li ve - nit im - pe - ri - o.
Tu - a re - gi lau - da - tur pro - bi - tas.
Per te so - lum cum no - bis pa - tu - it
Te Rex vo - cat ad su - am cu - ri - am.
E - ris, su - pra ut di - cit Da - ri - us.
Er - go ve - ni, iam o - mnis cu - ri - a

Ser - ve De - i no - stra le - ga - ti - o.
Te com - men - dat mi - ra cal - li - di - tas.
Sig - num dex - tre quod o - mnes la - tu - it.
Ut a - gnos - cat tu - am pru - den - ti - am.
Prin - ci - pa - lis con - si - li - a - ri - us.
Pre - pa - ra - tur ad tu - a gau - di - a.

Et Daniel:

G'en - vois al Roi.

Conductus Danielis:

Con - gau-den - tes ce - le-bre - mus na - ta - lis sol - lem - pni - a.
Iam de mor - te nos re - de - mit De - i sa - pi - en - ti - a.

Ho - mo na - tus est in car - ne, qui cre - a - vit o - mni - a.
Na - sci-tu - rum quem pre-di - xit pro - phe-te fa - cun - di - a.

Da - ni - e - lis iam ces - sa - vit un - cti - o - nis co - pi - a:
Ces - sat re - gni Iu - de - o - rum con - tu-max po - ten - ti - a.

In hoc na - ta - li - ti - o. Da - ni - el. cum gau - di - o

te lau-dat hec con - ti - o. Tu Su-san - nam li - be - ra - sti
Cum te De - us in - spi - ra - vit

de mor-ta - li cri - mi-ne. Tes - tes fal - sos com - pro-ba - sti
su - o san - cto fla - mi - ne. Bel dra - co - nem per - e - mi - sti

re - os ac - cu - sa - mi-ne. Et te De - us ob - ser-va - vit
co - ram ple - bis a - gmi-ne. Er - go sit laus De - i ver - bo

le - o - num vo - ra - gi - ne.
ge - ni - to de Vir - gi - ne.

Et Daniel Regi:

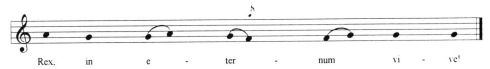

Rex, in e - ter - num vi - ve!

Cui Rex:

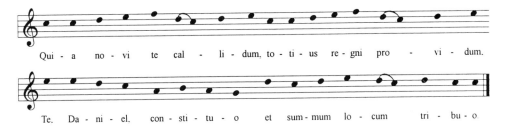

Qui - a no - vi te cal - li - dum, to - ti - us re - gni pro - vi - dum,

Te, Da - ni - el, con - sti - tu - o et sum - mum lo - cum tri - bu - o.

Et Daniel Regi:

Rex, mi - chi si cre - di - de - ris, per me nil ma - li fe - ce - ris.

Tunc Rex faciet eum sedere iuxta se, et alii consiliarii Danieli in-
videntes quia gratior erit Regi, aliis in consilium ductis ut Danielem
interficiant, dicent Regi:

Rex, in e - ter - num vi - ve!

Item:

De - cre - ve - runt in tu - a cu - ri - a prin - ci - pan - di qui - bus est
Si quis au - su tam te - me - ra - ri - o re - nu - e - rit tu - o con -

glo - ri - a, ut ad tu - i ri - go - rem no - mi - nis
si - li - o. Ut pre - ter te co - la - tur de - i - tas.

o - mni spre - to vi - go - re nu - mi - nis. per tri - gin - ta
iu - di - ci - i sit ta - lis fir - mi - tas. In le - o - num

di - e - rum spa - ti - um a - do - re - ris ut de - us
tra - da - tur fo - ve - am. Sic di - ca - tur per to - tam

1
o - mni - um. O Rex!

2
re - gi - am. O Rex!

Et Rex dicat:

E - go man - do et re - man - do Ne sit spre - tum hoc de - cre - tum. Ohez!

Daniel hoc audiens ibit in domum suam et adorabit Deum suum, quem emuli videntes, accurrent et dicent Regi:

Nun - quid, Da - ri, ob - ser - va - ri sta - tu - i - sti o - mni - bus.

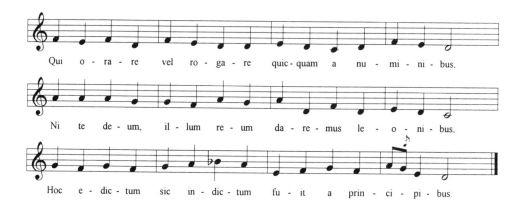

Qui o - ra - re vel ro - ga - re quic - quam a nu - mi - ni - bus.

Ni te de - um, il - lum re - um da - re - mus le - o - ni - bus.

Hoc e - dic - tum sic in - dic - tum fu - it a prin - ci - pi - bus.

Et Rex nesciens quare hoc dicerent respondet:

Ve - re ius - si me o - mni - bus a - do - ra - ri a gen - ti - bus.

Tunc illi adducentes Danielem, dicent Regi:

Hunc Iu - de - um su - um De - um Da - ni - e - lem vi - di - mus
A - do - ran - tem et pre - can - tem: tu - is spre - tis le - gi - bus.

Rex volens liberare Danielem, dicet:

Nun - quam vo - bis con - ce - da - tur, quod vir san - ctus sic per - da - tur.

Satrape hoc audientes ostendent ei legem, dicentes:

Lex Par-tho-rum et Me-do-rum iu-bet in an-na-li-bus.

ut qui spre-vit que de-cre-vit Rex. de-tur le-o-ni-bus.

Rex hoc audiens, velit nolit dicet:

Si spre-vit le-gem quam sta-tu-e-ram, Det pe-nas i-pse quas de-cre-ve-ram.

Tunc Satrape rapient Danielem, et ille respiciens Regem, dicet:

He-u! he-u! he-u! quo ca - su sor-tis ve-nit hec

da-mpna-ti-o mor-tis? He-u! he-u! he - u!

sce-lus in - fan-dum! Cur me da-bit ad la-ce-ran-dum

Hec fe-ra tur-ba fe - ris? Sic me. Rex. per-de-re que-ris?

He - u! qua mor-te mo-ri me co - gis! Par-ce fu-ro-ri!

Et Rex non valens eum liberare, dicet ei:

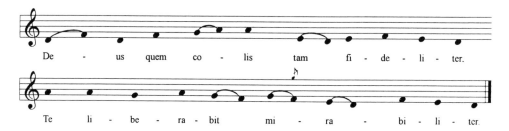

De - us quem co - lis tam fi - de - li - ter.

Te li - be - ra - bit mi - ra - bi - li - ter.

Tunc proicient Danielem in lacum; statimque angelus tenens gladium comminabitur leonibus ne tangant eum. Et Daniel intrans lacum dicet:

Hu - ius re - i non sum re - us: mi - se - re - re

me - i, De - us, e - le - y - son!

Mit - te De - us huc pa - tro - num qui re - fre - net

vim le - o - num: e - le - y - son.

Interea alius Angelus admonebit Abacuc prophetam ut deferat prandium quod portabat messoribus suis Danieli in lacum leonum dicens:

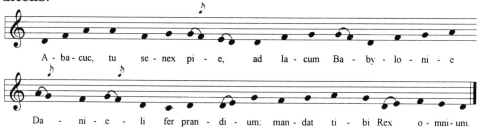

A - ba - cuc, tu se - nex pi - e, ad la - cum Ba - by - lo - ni - e

Da - ni - e - li fer pran - di - um: man - dat ti - bi Rex o - mni - um.

Cui Abacuc:

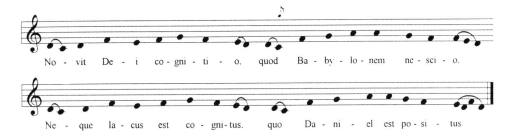

No - vit De - i co - gni - ti - o. quod Ba - by - lo - nem ne - sci - o.

Ne - que la - cus est co - gni - tus. quo Da - ni - el est po - si - tus.

Tunc Angelus apprehendens eum capillo capitis sui, ducet ad lacum, et Abacuc Danieli offerens prandium dicet:

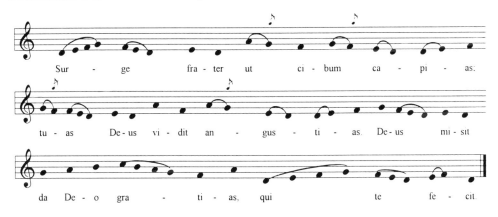

Sur - ge fra - ter ut ci - bum ca - pi - as.

tu - as De - us vi - dit an - gus - ti - as. De - us mi - sit

da De - o gra - ti - as. qui te fe - cit.

Et Daniel cibum accipiens, dicet:

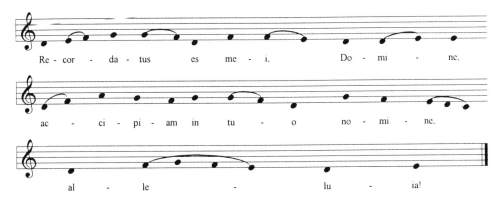

Re - cor - da - tus es me - i. Do - mi - ne.

ac - ci - pi - am in tu - o no - mi - ne.

al - le - lu - ia!

His transactis, Angelus reducet Abacuc in locum suum. Tunc Rex
descendens de solio suo veniet ad lacum, dicens lacrimabiliter:

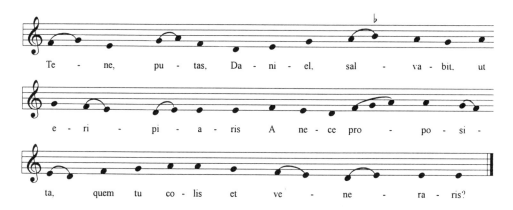

Te - ne, putas, Da - ni - el, sal - va - bit, ut
e - ri - pi - a - ris A ne - ce pro - po - si -
ta, quem tu co - lis et ve - ne - ra - ris?

Et Daniel Regi:

Rex, in e - ter - num vi - ve!

Item:

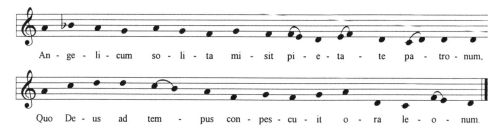

An - ge - li - cum so - li - ta mi - sit pi - e - ta - te pa - tro - num,
Quo De - us ad tem - pus con - pes - cu - it o - ra le - o - num.

Tunc Rex gaudens exclamabit:

Da - ni - e - lem e - du - ci - te, et e - mu - los im - mit - ti - te.

Cum expoliati fuerint et venerint ante lacum, clamabunt:

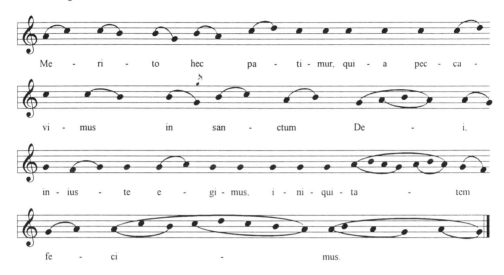

Me - ri - to hec pa - ti - mur, qui - a pec - ca -
vi - mus in san - ctum De - i.
in - ius - te e - gi - mus, i - ni - qui - ta - tem
fe - ci - mus.

Illi proiecti in lacum statim consumentur a leonibus. Et Rex videns hoc dicet:

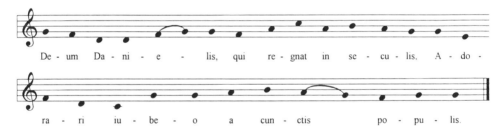

De - um Da - ni - e - lis, qui re - gnat in se - cu - lis. A - do -
ra - ri iu - be - o a cun - ctis po - pu - lis.

Daniel in pristinum gradum receptus, prophetabit:

Ec - ce ve - nit san - ctus il - le, san - cto - rum san - ctis - si - mus.
Ces - sant pha - na, ces - set re - gnum, ces - sa - bit et un - cti - o.
Quem rex i - ste iu - bet co - li po - tens et for - tis - si - mus.
In - stat re - gni Iu - de - o - rum fi - nis et op - pres - si - o.

Tunc angelus ex improviso exclamabit:

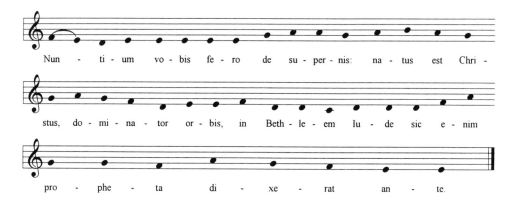

Nun - ti - um vo - bis fe - ro de su - per - nis: na - tus est Chri -

stus, do - mi - na - tor or - bis, in Beth - le - em Iu - de sic e - nim

pro - phe - ta di - xe - rat an - te.

His auditis cantores incipient: Te Deum laudamus.

FINIT DANIEL

The Play of Daniel
Translation

In your honor, Christ,
This play of Daniel
Was devised in Beauvais,
And it was the youth who made it.

While King Balthasar enters, his Princes sing this prosa *before him:*

To the Almighty,
Ruler of the stars,
This crowd of men and boys
Brings its praise.

For it hears that faithful Daniel
Staunchly suffered and endured
Many trials.

The King summoned wise men
Who might explain
The meaning of the letters
Written by that right hand.

Because the scribes could not explain them,
They stood silent there
Before the King.

But when Daniel read the writing,
What had been hidden to them
Was soon revealed.

When Balthasar saw how he surpassed the others,
He elevated him above them
In the court.

He was accused on an invented charge

And was sentenced
To be torn to pieces by the lions' mouth.

But, God, you wished
That those beasts who had previously been hostile
Would now be kind to Daniel.

To him also you sent bread
Delivered by an airborne prophet
So that he would not be hungry.

Then the King ascends his throne, and the Satraps, acclaiming him, say:

King, live forever!

And the King, opening his mouth says:

You who obey my words,
Bring for my use the [serving] vessels
My Father took from the temple
When he devastated Judea.

The Satraps, while bringing the vessels, sing this prosa *in honor of the King:*

Let us sing praise to our King,
    powerful and great
Let us sound forth worthy praise
    with able voices
Let the joyful crowd sing solemn
    hymns.

Let them play the harp and clap
their hands
And make a glad sound in a thou-
sand ways.

When his father destroyed the
temple of the Jews
He did a great deed,
And this King in his reign follows
his father's example.

His father looted the kingdom of
the Jews;
His son now embellishes his feasts
With their splendid vessels.

These are the royal vessels, stolen
from Jerusalem;
Now royal Babylon is enriched by
them.
Let us bring them to Balthasar,
our King,
Who has dressed his men in purple raiment.

He is mighty, he is strong, he is
glorious,
He is righteous, courteous, seemly,
and handsome.

Let us sing praises for so great a
King with euphonious voices,
Let us all sound forth together in
sonorous praise.

Laughing Babylon applauds, Jerusalem laments,
The latter is robbed, the former in
triumph venerates Balthasar.

So let us all rejoice in such great
power
While offering these royal vessels
to his majesty.

Then the Princes say:

See, here they are before you.

*Meanwhile, a right hand appears
before the King and writes on the
wall:* Mane, Techel, Phares. *On
seeing this, the King, astounded,
cries out:*

Call the Chaldean astrologers and
the soothsayers,
Seek out the diviners and bring
the wise men.

*Then the wise men are brought in,
who say to the King:*

King, live forever!
See, we attend upon you.

And the King:

Whoever can read this writing
And disclose its meaning
Will be given power over Babylon:
He will be dressed in purple
And wear a golden chain around
his neck.

*And they, not knowing how to de-
cipher the writing, say to the King:*

We can neither decipher this writing
Nor give advice on its meaning or
on the hand that wrote it.

Conductus *of the Queen, coming to
the King:*

While the learned and wise men
are assembled,
Tormenting their brains
But unable to tell

What the vision of the hand signi-
fies,
See, the royal consort comes,
She of wisdom and noble birth,
Rich and powerful,
Arrayed in golden garments.

She will bring forth
The hidden prophet,
By whose explanation
The King will learn
That it is his own downfall
That has been written here.
Therefore let this heroine be ac-
companied
With joyful applause;
Let strings and voices
Resound in sonorous music.

*Then the Queen upon her arrival
venerates the King and says:*

King, live forever!

Listen, King Balthasar, to my ad-
vice
So that you may come to know
The meaning of the writing.

*On hearing this, the King turns to
face the Queen; and the Queen
says:*

Together with the captive people
from Judea
A certain Daniel, who is learned
in prophetic riddles,
Was brought here from his homeland
As a consequence of your father's
victory.

Because he lives under your authority,
Reason requires that he should be

summoned.
Therefore give the order without
delay,
For he will teach you what is hidden in the vision.

Then the King says to his Princes:

Seek out Daniel,
And when you have found him,
bring him here.

*Then the Princes, having found
Daniel, say to him:*

Daniel, prophet of God, come to
the King,
Come, for he desires to speak with
you.
He is fearful and confused,
Daniel, come to the King!
He wants to learn from you what
is hidden to us.

He will enrich you with gifts—
Daniel, come to the King—
If he can learn from you what the
writing means.

And Daniel to them:

I greatly wonder on whose advice
The royal order summons me.
I will go, however, and through
me, without reward,
The obscure will be made known.

Conductus *of Daniel coming to the
King:*

Here is the true servant of God
Whom all people praise;
The fame of whose wisdom
Is known to the King's court.
Through us the King has sum-

moned him.

Daniel:

As a poor man and an exile, I go
    with you to the King.

Princes:

In the splendor of youth,
Full of heavenly grace,
He quite excels all others
In virtue, life, and character.
Through us the King has sum-
    moned him.

Daniel:

As a poor man and an exile, I go
    with you to the King.

Princes:

This is he by whose help
The writing of the right hand will
    be interpreted,
That vision which shook the King
    to the core.
Through us the King has sum-
    moned him.

Daniel:

As a poor man and an exile, I go
    with you to the King.

*When Daniel comes before the
King, he says to him:*

King, live forever!

And the King to Daniel:

Are you the one called Daniel,
Brought here with the wretched of

Judea?
They say that you possess the
    spirit of God
And have foreknowledge of what
    is hidden.
If therefore you can interpret the
    writing,
You will be enriched with innum-
    erable gifts.

And Daniel to the King:

King, I do not want your gifts;
I will explain the writing without
    reward.
The meaning is this:
Disaster hangs over you.

Your father, once powerful
Above all others,
And swollen overmuch with pride,
Was cast down from glory.

For he did not walk with God,
But made a god of himself;
He stole the vessels from the tem-
    ple
And used them for himself.

But after manifold foolish deeds
He finally lost his wealth;
Bereft of his human form,
Grass became his food.

And you, his son,
No less impious than he,
Follow the deeds of your father
And use these same vessels.

And as this is displeasing to God,
The time of his vengeance is at
    hand:
For the writing means
That punishment now threatens
    you.

"Mane," says the Lord:
This is the end of your reign;
"Techel" signifies the scales
In which you are weighed and
found wanting.
"Phares" means division:
Your kingdom will be given over
to another.

And the King:

Let him who thus brings to light
what was hidden
Be clothed in regal vestments.

*When Daniel, dressed in regal gar-
ments, is seated next to the King,
the King exclaims to the Prince of
his army:*

Take away the vessels, leader of
the troops,
Lest they be the cause of misery
to me.

*Then, having left the palace, the
Satraps return the vessels, and the
Queen departs.* Conductus *of the
Queen:*

In the book of Solomon
Worthy and due honor is given to
womankind.

She is valued as someone strong
Coming from afar, from the ends
of the earth.

Her husband trusts her in his
heart;
She is his treasure beyond wealth.

Let this woman be compared with
her
Whose support the King deserves.

For the eloquence of her words
Corrects the judgment of the
learned men.

And we, who because of this most
solemn day
Are granted the occasion for playing this play,
Let us devoutly give her praises
And let those who are from far
away come and sing with us.

Conductus *of those who bring the
vessels before Daniel:*

We, who bring back the vessels of
the King
Feared by the people of Judea,
Let us, while we give honor to
Daniel, rejoice
And give him worthy praise.

He predicted the downfall of the
King
When he deciphered the writing;
He proved the duplicity of the wit-
nesses
And thus liberated Susanna.
Let us rejoice
And give him worthy praise.

Babylon made him an exile
When it took the Jews captive;
Balthasar honored him.
Let us rejoice
And give him worthy praise.

He is a holy prophet of God;
The Chaldeans honor him
As well as the heathens and the
Jews;
Acclaiming him therefore,
Let us rejoice
And give him worthy praise.

*Suddenly King Darius appears
with his Princes; and his harp
players and Princes come before
him, singing this psalm:*

Behold King Darius
Comes with his Princes,
A noble man with all his nobles.

And his court
Resounds with joy,
And there is dancing all around.

He is admirable
And to be honored by all;
Empires are subject to him.

All honor the King
And worship him.

And Babylon, his homeland,
Fears him.

When he hurls his troops into the
    fray
He destroys the enemy forces
And smites the strong ones:
He is adorned
With honor and nobility.

This is the noble
King Darius of Babylon:
With dance let this crowd
Rejoice in him,
And joyously praise
His mighty deeds,
So worthy to be wondered at.

Let all of us rejoice together;
Let the drums resound, the harp-
    ists pluck their strings,
And the pipes of the musicians
    sound
To his honor.

*Before the King reaches his throne,
two men running ahead drive out
Balthasar as if killing him. Then,
when King Darius is seated in majesty, the court exclaims:*

King, live forever!

*Then two men, on bended knee,
secretly tell the King to summon
Daniel, and he orders him to be
brought. And they, admonishing
the others, speak as follows:*

Listen, Princes of the royal court
Who administer the laws of this
    whole country.

There is a certain wise man in
    Babylon
Who unveils secrets through the
    grace of the gods.

His counsel has pleased the King
Because he once interpreted the
    writing to Balthasar.

Now go quickly, let there be no
    delay,
Because we want to ask for his
    advice.

Let him, if he comes, be made the
    counselor
Of the King and the third man in
    the kingdom.

*Having found Daniel, the envoys
say this on behalf of the King:*

Servant of God, our legation
    comes
Because of a royal order.

Your virtue has been praised be-

fore the King,
And your wondrous wisdom re-
commends you.

Only through you was the sign of
the right hand,
A mystery to all, explained to us.

The King summons you to his
court
To acknowledge your wisdom.

You will be, so King Darius said,
The first among his counselors.

Therefore come! already the whole
court
Is prepared to welcome you.

And Daniel:

I'll go to the King.

Conductus *of Daniel:*

Let us together joyfully celebrate
the solemn feast of the Nativity;
God's wisdom has now redeemed
us from death.

He who created everything has
been born as man in the flesh;
The eloquent words of the prophet
predicted that he would be
born.
As Daniel foresaw, the power of
anointing has ceased,
And the stubborn power of the
kingdom of the Jews ceases.

On this feast of the Nativity,
Daniel, this crowd honors you
with joy.
You freed Susanna of the deadly

accusation
When God inspired you with his
holy spirit.
You proved the false witnesses
guilty of their own charge.

You slew Bel the Dragon in front
of the assembled people;
God kept watch over you in the
lions' den;
Therefore praise be to the Word of
God, born of the Virgin.

And Daniel to the King:

King, live forever!

The King to him:

Because I know that you are wise
And watchful over the whole king-
dom,
Daniel, I select you
And assign you to the highest
place.

And Daniel to the King:

King, if you have trust in me,
Through me you will do nothing
wrong.

*Then the King causes him to sit
next to him. And the other Counselors, growing envious of Daniel
because he is more loved by the
King, and having drawn others
into a conspiracy to kill Daniel,
say to the King:*

King, live forever!

Also:

Those to whom belongs the glory

of ruling
Have decreed in your court
That to enforce the rigor of your
    name
All divine power should be
    spurned,
And during the space of thirty
    days
You should be worshipped as the
    god of all,
O King.

If anyone should be so bold
As to oppose your order,
So that a deity other than yourself
    is worshipped,
Let him undergo this stern judg-
    ment:
Let him be thrown into the lions'
    den.
May this be known throughout the
    kingdom,
O King.

And the King says:

I order and confirm
That this decree must not be
    scorned.
Hear ye!

*On hearing this, Daniel goes into
his house and worships his God.
When they see this, those who envy
him run to the King and say to
him:*

Darius, have you not promulgated
    a decree
To be followed by everyone:
That if anyone prays to or be-
    seeches one of the gods
And does not acknowledge you to
    be god,
Then we should give that guilty

one to the lions?
This decree has been thus pro-
    claimed
By the Princes.

*The King, not knowing why they
say this, answers:*

Truly, I ordered that I
Shall be worshipped by all peo-
    ples.

*Then they bring in Daniel and say
to the King:*

We saw this Jew, Daniel,
Worshipping and praying to his
    own God
In contempt of your laws.

*The King, wishing to free Daniel,
says:*

May it never be permitted to you
To have this man killed in such a
    way.

*The Satraps, on hearing this, show
him the law, saying:*

The law of the Parthians and
    Medes
Demands in its annals
That he who disobeys what the
    King has ordered
Shall be given to the lions.

*On hearing this, the King says,
willy-nilly:*

If he has disobeyed the law that I
    enacted,
Let him pay the penalty that I de-
    creed.

Then the Satraps seize Daniel, and he, looking at the King, says:

Alas, alas, alas — by what fate
Has come this condemnation to death?
Alas, alas, alas — unspeakable wickedness!
Why will this savage crowd
Hand me over to be mauled by savage beasts?
Is it thus, O King, that you seek to destroy me?

Alas, what kind of death
Do you force me to die?
Temper your rage.

And the King, unable to set him free, says to him:

The God whom you worship so faithfully
Will set you free by a miracle.

Then they throw Daniel into the lions' den; and immediately an Angel, holding a sword, prevents the lions from touching him. As Daniel enters the den, he says:

I am innocent of this crime;
Have mercy on me, O God:
Eleison!
Send, O God, a protector here
Who will curb the strength of the lions:
Eleison!

Meanwhile, another Angel instructs the prophet Habakkuk to take the meal that he was carrying to his reapers to Daniel in the lions' den, saying:

Habakkuk, you pious old man,
Take this meal
To the den in Babylon, to Daniel:
Thus the King of all commands you.

Habakkuk replies to him:

To the omniscience of God it is known
That I know neither Babylon,
Nor the den
In which Daniel was thrown.

Then, the Angel, grasping him by the hair of his head, leads him to the den, and Habakkuk says, as he offers Daniel the meal:

Rise, brother, and take this food;
God has seen your troubles.
God has sent this, give thanks to God
Who created you.

And Daniel, taking the food, says:

Lord, you have remembered me;
I will accept it in your name,
Alleluia.

When this has been done, the Angel takes Habakkuk back to his place. Then the King, getting down from his throne, comes to the den, and tearfully says:

Daniel, do you think that he whom you worship and honor
Will save you and snatch you away from your intended death?

And Daniel to the King:

King, live forever!

And also:

With his accustomed mercy God
     has sent an angelic protector
By whom he has restrained the
     jaws of the lions just in time.

Then the King cries out joyfully:

Bring Daniel out of the den
And throw in the envious men!

*When they have been stripped and
have come before the den, they cry
out:*

Deservedly we suffer this, because
     we have sinned
Against the holy man of God.
We have acted unjustly, and have
     committed grave fault.

*After they have been thrown into
the den, they are immediately con-
sumed by the lions. The King, on
seeing this, says:*

I order that the God of Daniel
Who reigns forever

Shall be worshipped by all.

*Daniel, restored to his former rank,
prophesies:*

See, that Holy One comes, the
     holiest of holies,
Whom this strong and powerful
King orders to be worshipped.

Temples cease, the kingdom is to
     cease,
Anointings also will be no more.
The end and overthrow of the
     kingdom of the Jews is at
     hand.

Then an Angel suddenly exclaims:

I bring you a message from high
     heaven:
Christ is born, Ruler of the world,
In Bethlehem of Judea, as the pro-
     phet foretold.

On hearing this, the cantors *begin
singing* Te Deum laudamus.

*—Translation by A. Marcel J.
Zijlstra (revised by Timothy
Graham)*

Index

Abraham 55
Abelard 18, 45
acting 20–21, 23–24, 26–27
Adam, Anglo-Norman play of 25, 40, 43, 58
Adelaide of Savoy 47
Adele of Champagne 47–48, 60
American Medieval Players 70
anointing 6, 42
Antichrist 38
   play of, at Tegernsee 21; *see also Coming of Antichrist*
Antigone, by Anouilh 70
Apocalypse 42, 56
apocryphal elements 35–37
architecture, church 12–15, 22–23, 30, 71–72
artisanship 19–20
Atkinson, Brooks 65
Aubry, Pierre 63
Auden, W. H. 64, 69
Augustine, St. 39, 55–56, 58
Aurelian of Réôme 85
authority, sacred and secular 37, 41, 44, 48–50, 52–53
Axton, Richard 58–59

Babylon 6, 35–38, 41–42, 49–50, 52, 58, 60
Baldwin, John 34
Ballard, Mary Anne 67
Balthasar (Belshazzar) 7, 14, 22, 24–28, 30, 35, 41–43, 46–52, 60, 81–82
   processions of 14, 51, 79
   and sacred vessels 6, 13, 46–47, 49–52, 77, 82
   as secular authority 41, 48–

50, 79
Barking, play at 26
Basse-Oeuvre 6, 11, 12–15, 18–21, 30; *see also* Beauvais Cathedral
Beauvais, commune of 46–47
Beauvais, community of 2–3, 7, 17–20, 39
   history of 45–46, 59
   ideology of 34, 41, 44–52
Beauvais Cathedral 1, 6, 11, 20, 34, 44, 48, 50–54, 59, 77, 84
   altar of Daniel at 21
   bishop's throne at 22, 51
   cathedral school at 1–2, 17–18, 27, 33, 59
Beck, Jean 63
Bel, idol 37, 55
Bel and the Dragon 55, 78
Belshazzar; *see* Balthasar
Benediktbeuern manuscript, plays included in 22, 25, 27
Benjamin, Walter 5
Bernard of Clairvaux 36, 49
Bevington, David 30, 47, 59–60
Bhabha, Homi K. 49
Bielitz, Mathias 81
bishop-counts 45–47, 49, 52–53, 60
Bishop's University, Lennoxville 68
Blanche of Castille 46, 53
Boston Camerata 68–69
Bourgeault, Cynthia 58, 67
Bowles, E. A. 89
boy bishop 16
Bressler, Charles 69
Browne, E. Martin 12, 14

Bullough, D. A. 50

Cain and Abel 25
Capetian dynasty 34–35
Cargill, Oscar 57
Carmina Burana; *see* Benedikt-
  beuern Manuscript
Chami, Émile 12–14, 19
Christ 35, 38, 40, 43, 48, 55–56,
  58
    prophecies concerning 5–6,
    15–16, 38–42, 58, 78, 83
Christ ist erstanden 9
Christ the King, Cathedral of,
  Kalamazoo 3, 5, 71, 73
Christmas 15–16, 18, 21, 24, 25–
  27, 39–41, 43, 52, 59, 77–78
churches, architecture of 12–15,
  22–23, 30, 71–72
Church of the Transfiguration
  (Little Church Around the Cor-
  ner, New York City) 9, 73
Circumcision, Feast of 16–18, 20,
  39, 77
    Office of 16, 44, 57, 59–60,
    79–80
City of God, by St. Augustine 56,
  58
Clerkes of Oxenford 11, 67
Cloisters, The 12, 65, 71
Cohen, Joel 68–69
Collins, Fletcher, Jr. 3, 7, 51, 68,
  85, 89
comedy, in *Daniel* 15
Coming of Antichrist, Chester
  play of 38
conductus 20, 64, 78, 80–81
*Contra Judaeos, Paganos, et Ari-
  anos*, pseudo-Augustinian sermon 39–40, 58
costumes 65–66
counsellors 23, 36, 43, 48–50,
  58, 83–84
Coussemaker, Edmond de 63, 77,
  89

dance 4, 83
Daniel 15, 56, 79, 81, 83
    in book of *Daniel* 36–37
    house of 13, 21–22, 71
    as prophet 5–6, 15, 36–40,
    42, 49, 83–84
    and secular authority 48, 51–
    52, 55
    youth of 2, 9, 36, 39, 57

Daniel, book of 34–40, 55–57, 78
Daniel, The Play of (*Ludus Dani-
  elis*)
    action in 25–27
    date of 11, 45, 59, 85
    modern productions of 1–7, 8,
    11–12, 63–71
    staging of 1, 3, 7, 11–32,
    50–51, 58, 71–72
    text of 4, 64, 69, 78, 89–90
    transcriptions of 4, 8, 89–90
Darius 17, 21–24, 26–27, 38, 40–
  42, 47–50, 61, 78, 82–84, 89
    invasion of 15, 24, 35, 42, 82
    law of 36, 49, 83–84
    as secular authority 41, 48–
    49, 50
Davidson, Audrey Ekdahl 3, 7,
  71
Davidson, Clifford 8, 71
Doob, Penelope 55
dragon 37, 55, 78
drama, liturgical
    settings for 22–23, 30, 71–72
    terminology in 24–25, 31
dreams 36–37

Early Music 67
Early Music Consort of London
  67
Early Music Ensemble, of Univer-
  sity of California, Davis 67
Easter plays 22, 25–27, 31, 66
Edinbugh Festival 69, 72

Egerton MS. 2615 4, 8, 11, 31, 54, 77, 80, 85, 89
  Circumcision Office in 16–17, 39, 77, 79–80
  and modern productions 63–64, 67
Emmerson, Richard K. 2, 7, 28
empires, four 38, 56
Ensemble for Early Music, New York 68–69, 72
Epiphany Office 79
Epstein, Marcia 59
Essen, Cathedral of 27
exegesis, medieval 35–39, 43–44, 52

faith 2, 55
Fallis, David 73
Fassler, Margot 17, 23, 28, 33, 43–44, 49, 57, 59–61, 65–66, 73, 77, 80
Feast of Fools 16, 23, 33, 44, 49, 52, 57, 59–61, 66, 70, 73, 80
  reform of 16–17, 44, 52, 59, 77
fiery furnace, three youths in 36, 40, 48–49
Fish, Stanley 54
Flanigan, C. Clifford 19, 29, 33, 52–53, 57
Fleury Playbook 21, 25–27, 66
Folger Consort 68, 72
folktale elements 35–37
France 5, 34–35, 49, 52–53, 60
  monarchy of 7, 45–46, 48, 50–51, 54
Frank, Grace 59
Freeman, Margaret 65
French language 2, 4, 19, 54, 81

Garlande, Stephen de 45
Grand Theatre, Warsaw 70
Grandes Chroniques de France 48
Greenberg, Noah 7, 12, 63–68, 71–73, 77, 89

Gregory IX 54, 85
Guido of Arezzo 78, 85
Guy of Beauvais, Bishop 45
Guyotjeannin, Olivier 60

Habakkuk 6, 15, 21–22, 37, 42, 57, 78, 84
Harris-Taylor, Carol 68
Harrowing of Hell 43, 58
Haskell, Harry 66
Helinand, chronicle of 59
Henry of France, Bishop 45, 47, 49
Herod, plays of 26, 49, 66
  character of 21
Hilarius 18, 19, 24, 39, 45, 48, 57, 59–61
Hildebrand, Paul 68–69
Hiley, David 85–86
Historia pontificalis, by John of Salisbury 47
Hogwood, Christopher 67
Holoman, D. Kern 67
Hughes, Andrew 12

ideology 33, 44–53
  theocratic 34–35, 41, 44–45, 49, 51–53
Innocents, Feast of 16, 77
International Congress on Medieval Studies, Kalamazoo 3, 89
irony 7
Isaac, Vorau play of 25

Jerome 37, 47, 55–56, 60
Jerusalem 6, 50–52, 77
Jews 5–6, 42
Job 55
Jocelin, bishop of Soisson 47
John of Salisbury 47
John, St., Apostle 26
  Feast of 16, 77
Joseph, play of, from Laon 21
Josephus 60
Jubilemus cordis voce 79

Killing of the Innocents, Fleury
  play of 66
Kirstein, Lincoln 64
Klausner, David 73
Kornbluth, Genevra 55

Lamentations of Jeremiah 69
Last Judgment 42–43, 58
Lawrence of Durham 55
Lazarus, play of 25
Lecky, Steven 68
lighting 23, 65, 72
lions' den 21, 23–24, 30, 36–37,
  41–42, 58, 73, 78, 84
    in modern productions 24, 71,
    73
    position of 21–22, 30
Little Church Around the Corner;
  see Church of the Transfigura-
  tion
liturgical calendar 11, 15–17, 77
Louis VI 46–47
Louis VII 35, 45–48
Louis VIII 45
Louis IX 35, 46, 54
Ludus Danielis; *see Daniel, The
  Play of*
Ludus Paschalis, from Tours 27

Margaret of Provence 54, 85
Martin of Léon 38
Mary Magdalene 25–27
McGee, Timothy 68
Medieval Music-Drama News 66
melody 19, 78–81, 83–84
Metropolitan Museum of Art 68–
  69
Miles of Nanteuil, Bishop 45–47,
  53, 57
monarchy 7, 35, 41, 45–46, 48–
  49, 50–53
Montpellier Christmas play 21
Munich Psalter 58
Munrow, David 67
Murray, Stephen 14, 45, 59

music 20, 77–86
  in modern productions 1–5,
  7–8, 64, 66, 69, 70, 73, 89–90
  secular 19, 73
musical instruments 30, 71, 73,
  82–83
musical notation 20, 63, 78, 85–
  86, 89–90

Nafziger, Kenneth 70
National Cathedral, Washington,
  D.C. 65, 72
Nativity, prophecies of 38–39,
  41, 43, 78
Nebuchadnezzar 6, 35–36, 40,
  42, 49, 51, 55, 81
New York Pro Musica 12, 14, 63,
  65–66, 69–71, 77
Noah 55
Notre-Dame Cathedral, Paris 53
Nuntium vobis fero de supernis
  8, 16

Oakshott, Jane 66
Officium Circumcisionis; *see* Cir-
  cumcision, Office of
Ogden, Dunbar H. 73
Ordo prophetarum 39–40, 57–58
Ordo Rachelis 27
Ordo repraesentationis Adae; *see
  Adam*, Anglo-Norman play of
Orientis partibus (*Prose of the
  Ass*) 17, 23, 31, 58, 79–80
Origen 60
ornamentation, on *Basse-Oeuvre*
  13–14, 19–20
Owens, Melody S. 73

Park Place Baptist Church, Nor-
  folk 70
Parry, David 68
Paschal II, Pope 45
Peregrinus 22, 25
Peter, St. 26, 53

Philip Augustus 35, 45–46, 48
Philip I 45
Philip of Dreux, Bishop 45–46
Poculi Ludique Societas 68, 73
poetic forms 19, 80, 85
Poland 69, 70
politics 45–46, 60
Porphyry 60
Porter, Andrew 69
prayer, gestures of 26, 31
priests 77
Procession of the Prophets; *see
   Ordo Prophetarum*
processions 6, 14–15, 20–21, 23,
   73, 78, 81, 84–85
prophecies 5, 6, 15–16, 38–44,
   49, 58, 78, 83
Prophets of Antichrist, Chester
   play of 38
Prophets, Towneley play of 38
Prose of the Ass; *see Orientis par-
   tibus*
Psacharopoulos, Nikos 12, 64

Queen 14, 20–21, 30–31, 40, 42,
   47–48, 50, 58–59, 60, 64, 80–82
Queen Mary Road Church, Montreal 68

Racine, Jean Baptiste 2
Ralph of Beauvais 18, 45, 59
Ramm, Andrea von 69
Rankin, Susan 19
Rastall, Richard 66
Reaney, Gilbert 54
Reese, Gustave 63
reform 16–17, 44, 52, 59, 77
Regularis Concordia 31
Renz, Frederick 68
rhythm 1, 24, 64, 78, 80–85, 89
Romanesque cathedral at Beau-
   vais; *see Basse-Oeuvre*
Root of Jesse, N-town play of 38
Rouen Cathedral 22
rubrics 4, 9, 20–22, 24–27

Rupert of Deutz 37, 55–56, 58

St. Denis, abbey of 35, 46–47, 53
St. John the Baptist, Cathedral
   of, Charleston 69
St. John the Divine, Cathedral of,
   New York 68–69
St. John the Evangelist, Cathe-
   dral of, Milwaukee 70
Saint-Denis, Michel 2–3
salvation history 34, 52, 55
Satanowski, Robert 70
Schapiro, Meyer 65
Schola Cantorum "Quem Quaeri-
   tis" 3, 5, 8, 73
Schultze, Andrew 70
Sephardic chant 69
sets, theatrical 65, 71
Shakespeare, William 2
Silos Bible 31
singing 1, 4, 23, 27, 79–83;
   see also melody; music
Smithsonian Institution, Baird
   Hall at 72
Smoldon, William L. 16, 19, 66,
   85–86
social utility 41
Society for Old Music 71
Somniale Danielis 37
Son of Getron, The 25
Southern Baptist Theological
   Seminary Collegium Musicum
   67
space, theatrical 2, 6–7, 20–21,
   50–51, 71–72
Spiegel, Gabrielle 54
Spoleto Festival, Charleston,
   South Carolina 69
Spoleto Festival (Italy) 68
stage directions 2, 20–21, 23–27
Steel, Matthew 71
Stephen, St., Feast of 16, 77
Stevens, John 59, 78–79
subdeacons 16–17, 23, 77, 80

Suger, Abbot of St. Denis 35, 47, 54
Susanna 37, 48, 55

Taylor, Jerome 12–13, 39, 65, 67, 78, 80
Te Deum laudamus 4, 5, 17, 40, 69, 84
theocratic ideology 34–35, 41, 44, 45, 49, 51, 52–53
throne 21, 30, 42, 51, 71
timing 24
Toronto Consort 73
Trinity-St. Paul's United Church, Toronto 73
troubadour-trouvère music 3, 63
Tydeman, William 59

University of California, Davis, Early Music Ensemble 67
University of Leeds, *Daniel* at 66
University of Pennsylvania Collegium Musicum 67

vernacular language 2, 4, 19, 54, 81

vessels, sacred 6, 13, 46, 52, 77, 80, 82
Victimae Paschali 27
Virgil 38
Visitatio Sepulchri 9, 22, 25–27, 31, 66, 73

wall, handwriting on the, by mysterious hand 24–25, 27, 36, 41, 43, 49–51, 73, 80–81
Warning, Rainer 44
Weakland, Rembert 63–66, 70, 89
Western Michigan University Collegium Musicum 71
Wilkins, Jay 67
Wondrous Love 69
Wulstan, David 12, 16, 18, 30, 67

Young, Karen 68
Young, Karl 17–19, 53, 57, 59, 89

Zijlstra, A. Marcel J. 4, 8, 73, 85–86

1. *Ludus Danielis.* "Incipit *Danielis Ludus.*" Egerton MS. 2615, fol. 95ʳ.

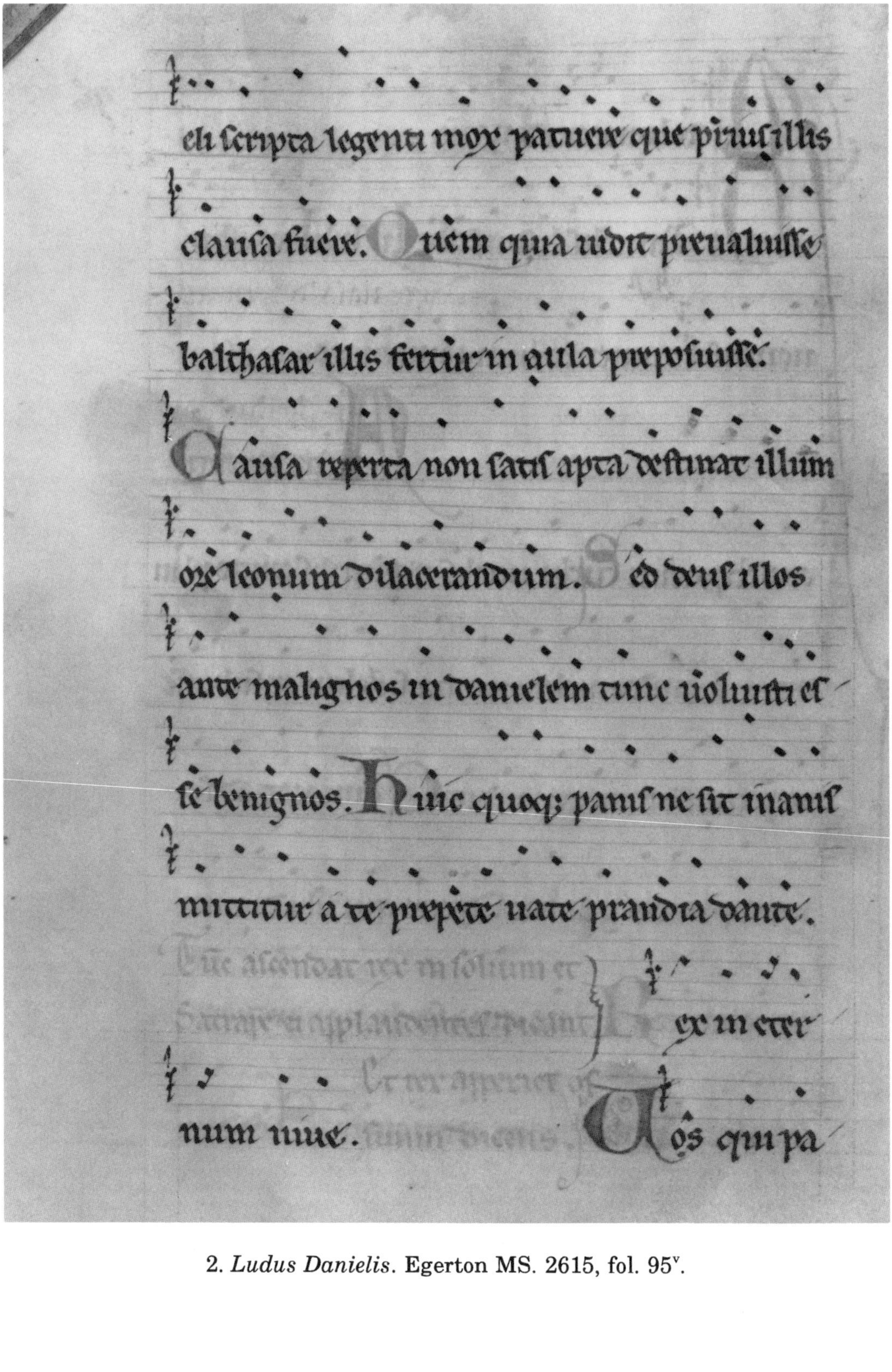

2. *Ludus Danielis*. Egerton MS. 2615, fol. 95v.

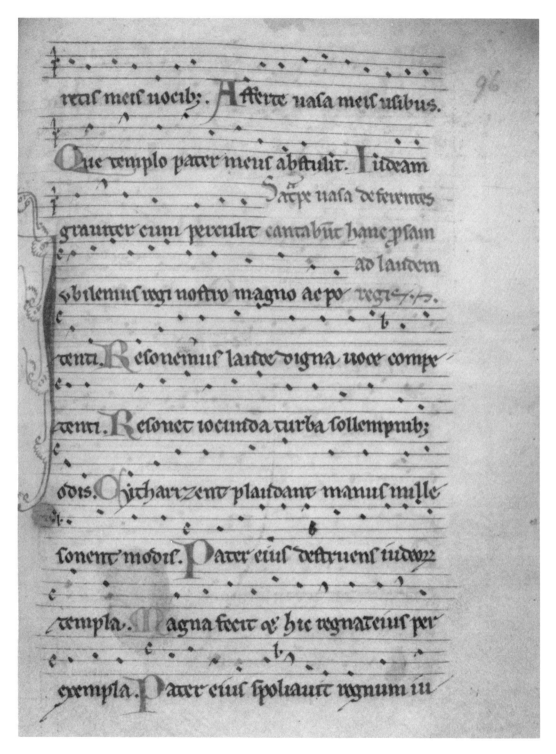

3. *Ludus Danielis*. Egerton MS. 2615, fol. 96ʳ.

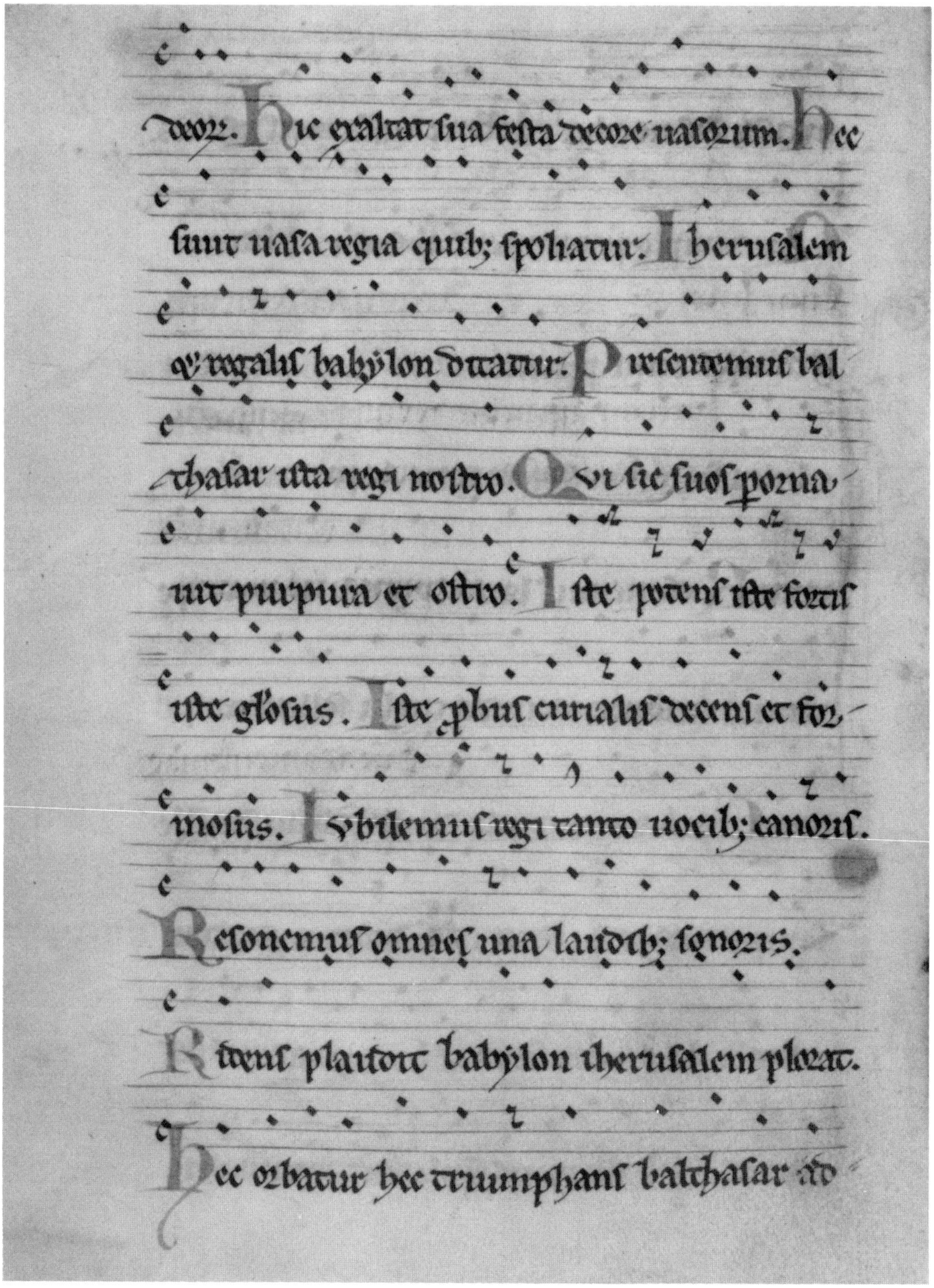

4. *Ludus Danielis*. Egerton MS. 2615, fol. 96v.

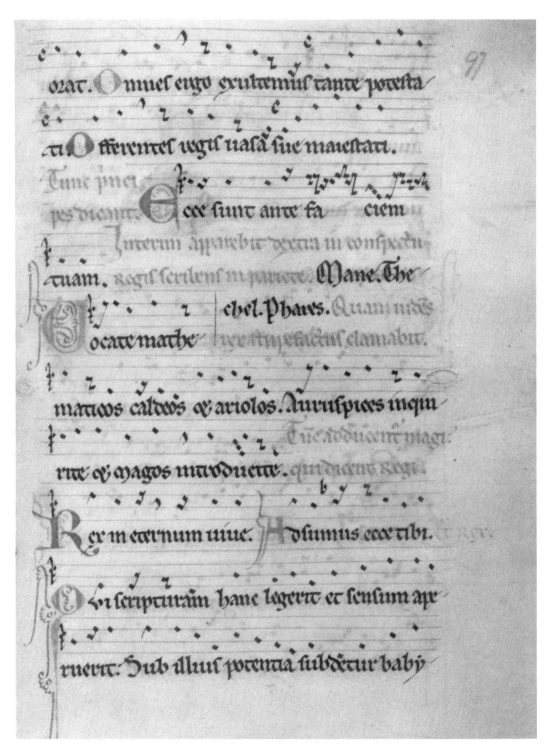

5. *Ludus Danielis*. The mysterious handwriting appears. Egerton MS. 2615, fol. 97[r].

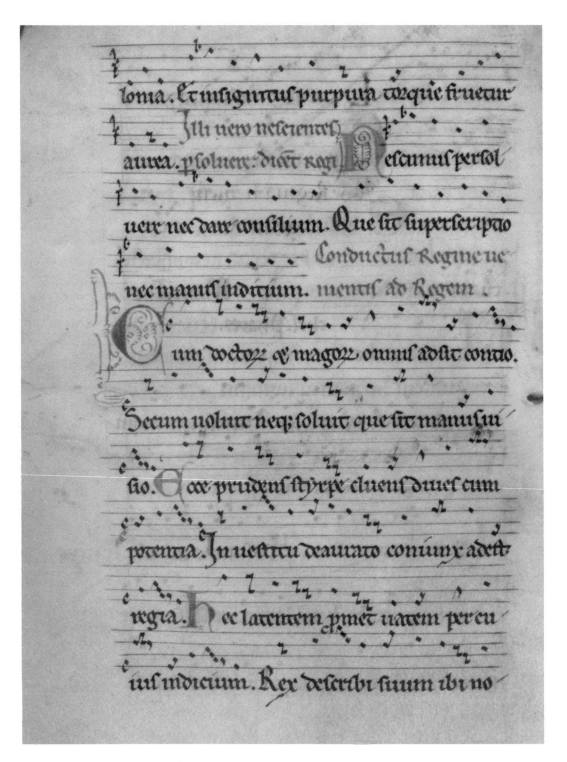

6. *Ludus Danielis*. Egerton MS. 2615, fol. 97ᵛ.

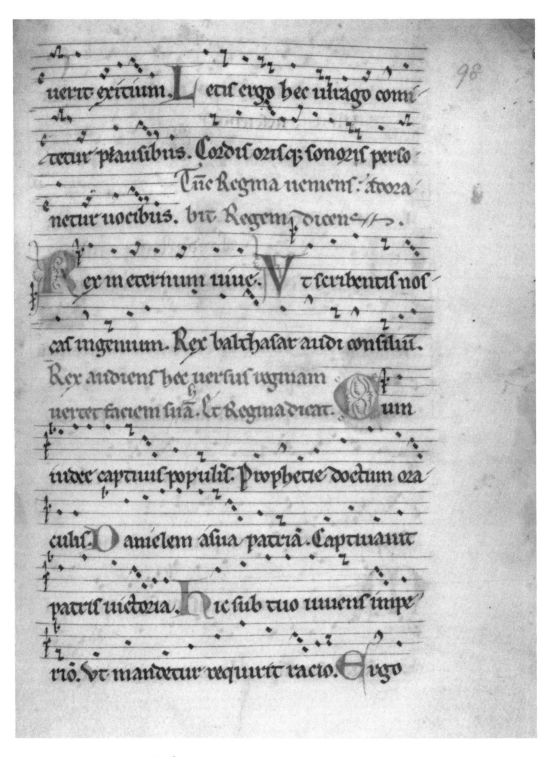

7. *Ludus Danielis*. Egerton MS. 2615, fol. 98^r.

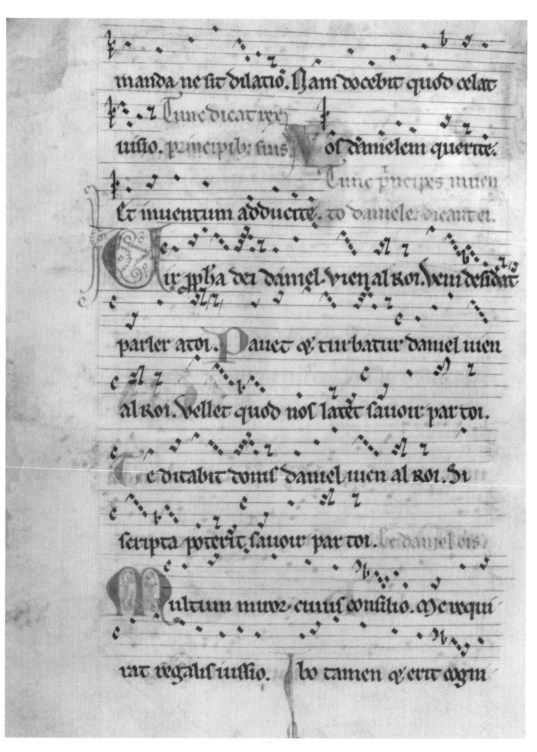

8. *Ludus Danielis*. Egerton MS. 2615, fol. 98ᵛ.

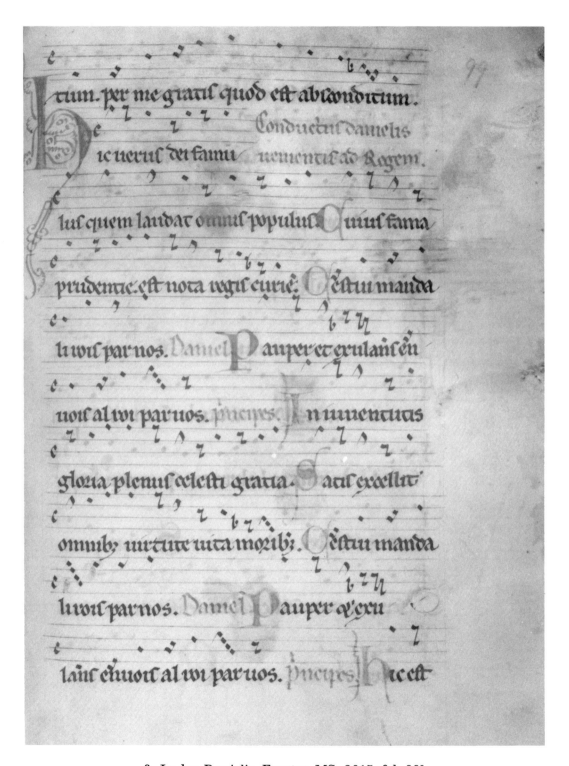

9. *Ludus Danielis*. Egerton MS. 2615, fol. 99^r.

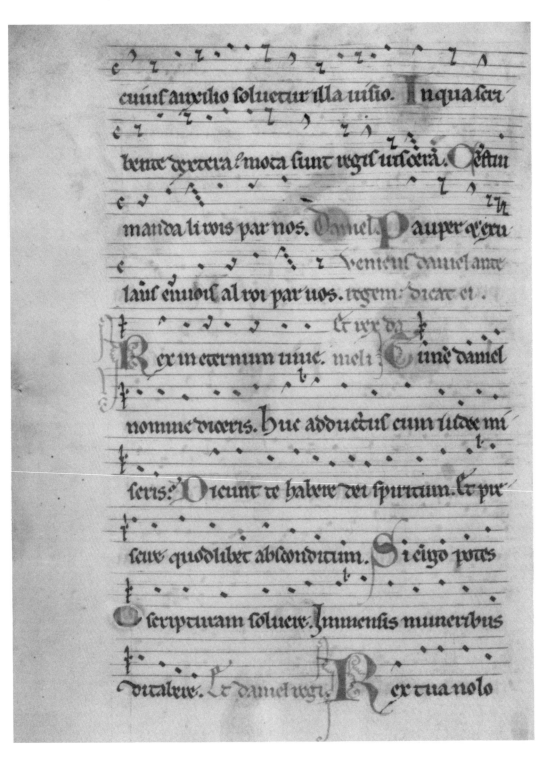

10. *Ludus Danielis*. Egerton MS. 2615, fol. 99ᵛ.

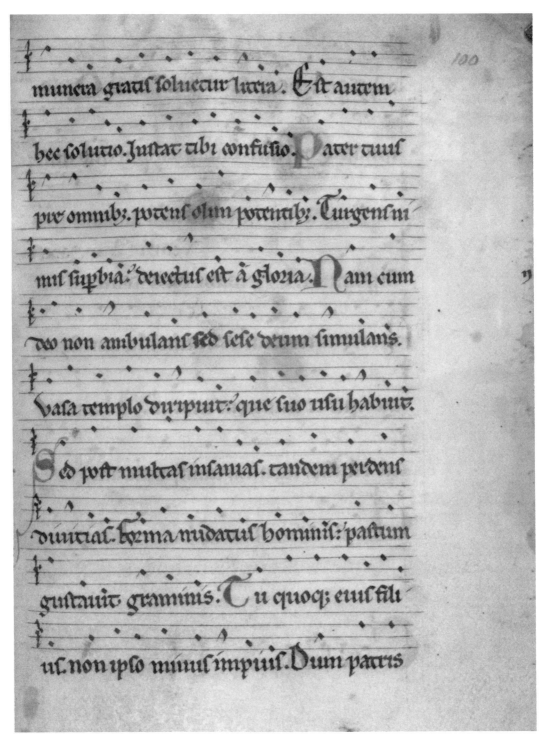

11. *Ludus Danielis*. Egerton MS. 2615, fol. 100[r].

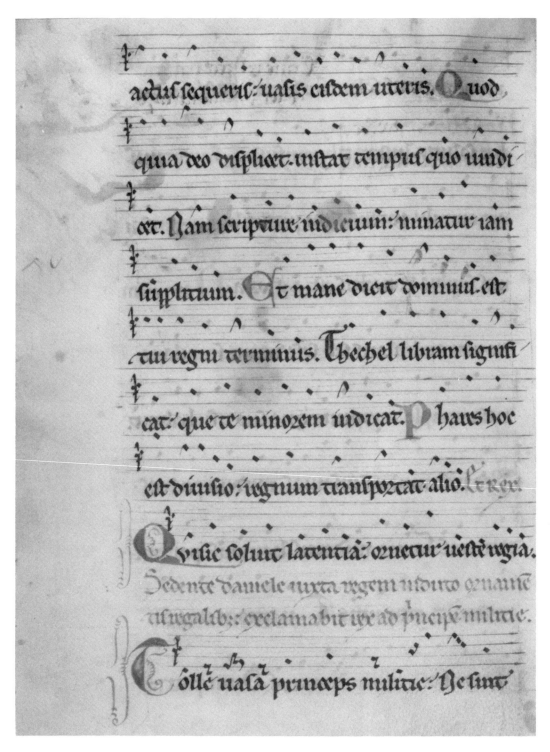

12. *Ludus Danielis*. Daniel explains the handwriting. Egerton MS. 2615, fol. 100ᵛ.

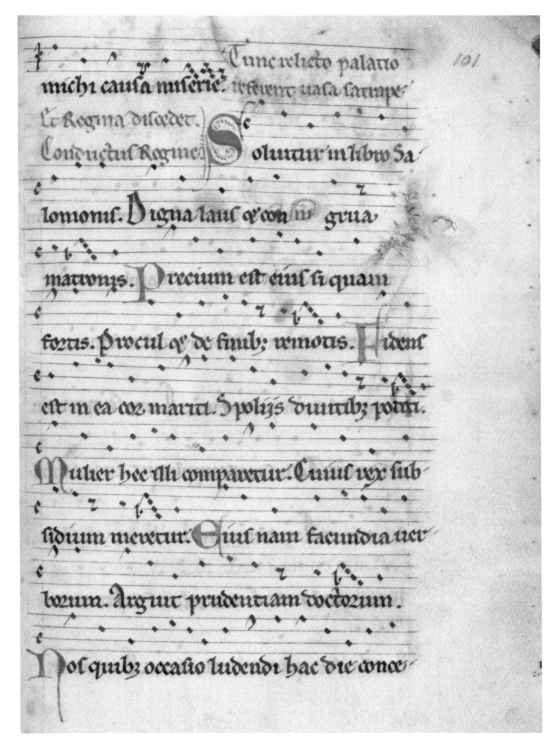

13. *Ludus Danielis*. Egerton MS. 2615, fol. 101ʳ.

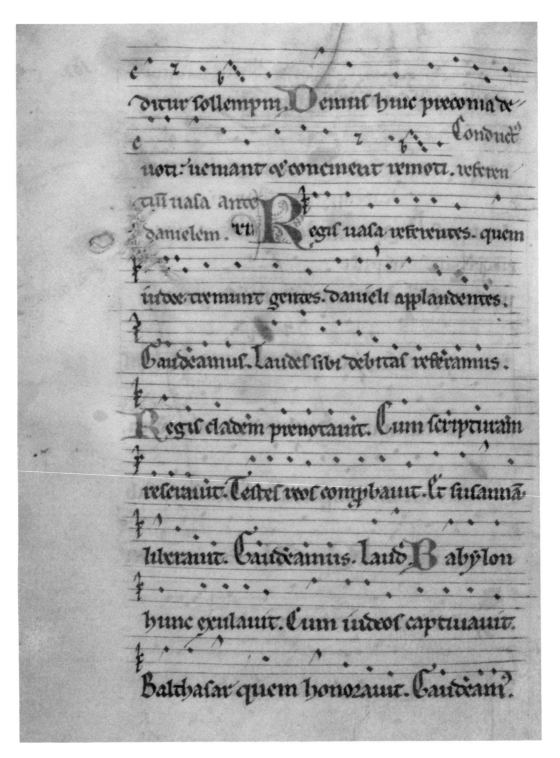

14. *Ludus Danielis*. Egerton MS. 2615, fol. 101ᵛ.

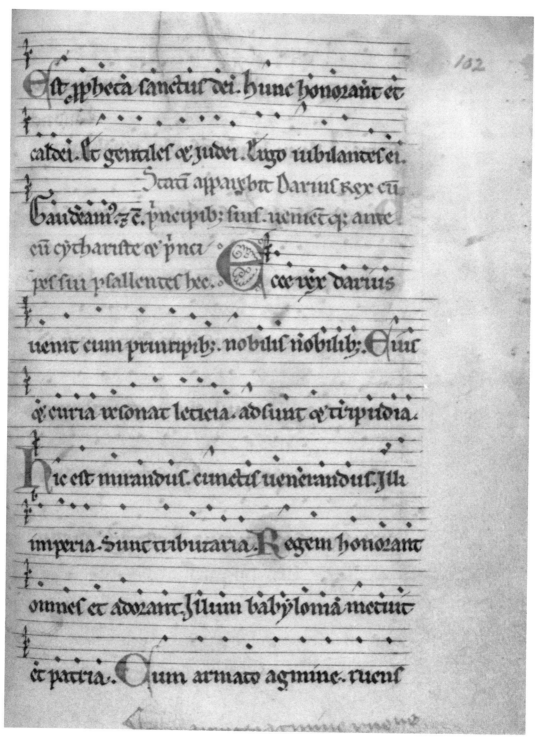

15. *Ludus Danielis.* Egerton MS. 2615, fol. 102^r.

et cum turbine. sternit cohortes. consurgit et

fortes. Illum honestas colit et nobilitas.

Hic est babylonius nobilis rex darius. Illi

cum tripudio. gaudeat hec contio. laudet

et cum gaudio. Eius facta fortia tam ad

mirabilia. Simul omnes gratulemur.

resonent et tympana. Cythariste tangant

cordas musicorum organa. Resonent ad eius

Antequam veniat rex ad solium suum

preconia. duo penitentes expellent baltha

sar quasi insufficientesecum. Tunc sedente

Dario rege in maiestate sua. Curia exclamabit.

16. *Ludus Danielis*. Darius overthrows Balthasar. Egerton MS. 2615, fol. 102ᵛ.

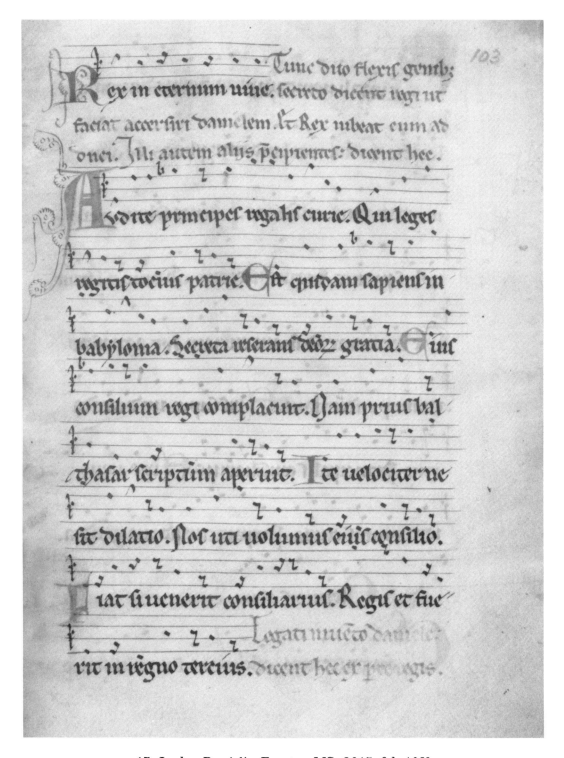

17. *Ludus Danielis*. Egerton MS. 2615, fol. 103^r.

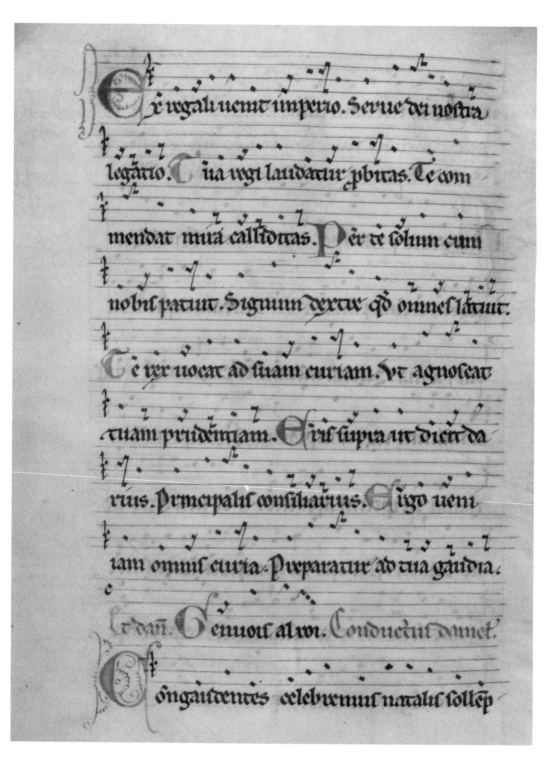

18. *Ludus Danielis*. Egerton MS. 2615, fol. 103ᵛ.

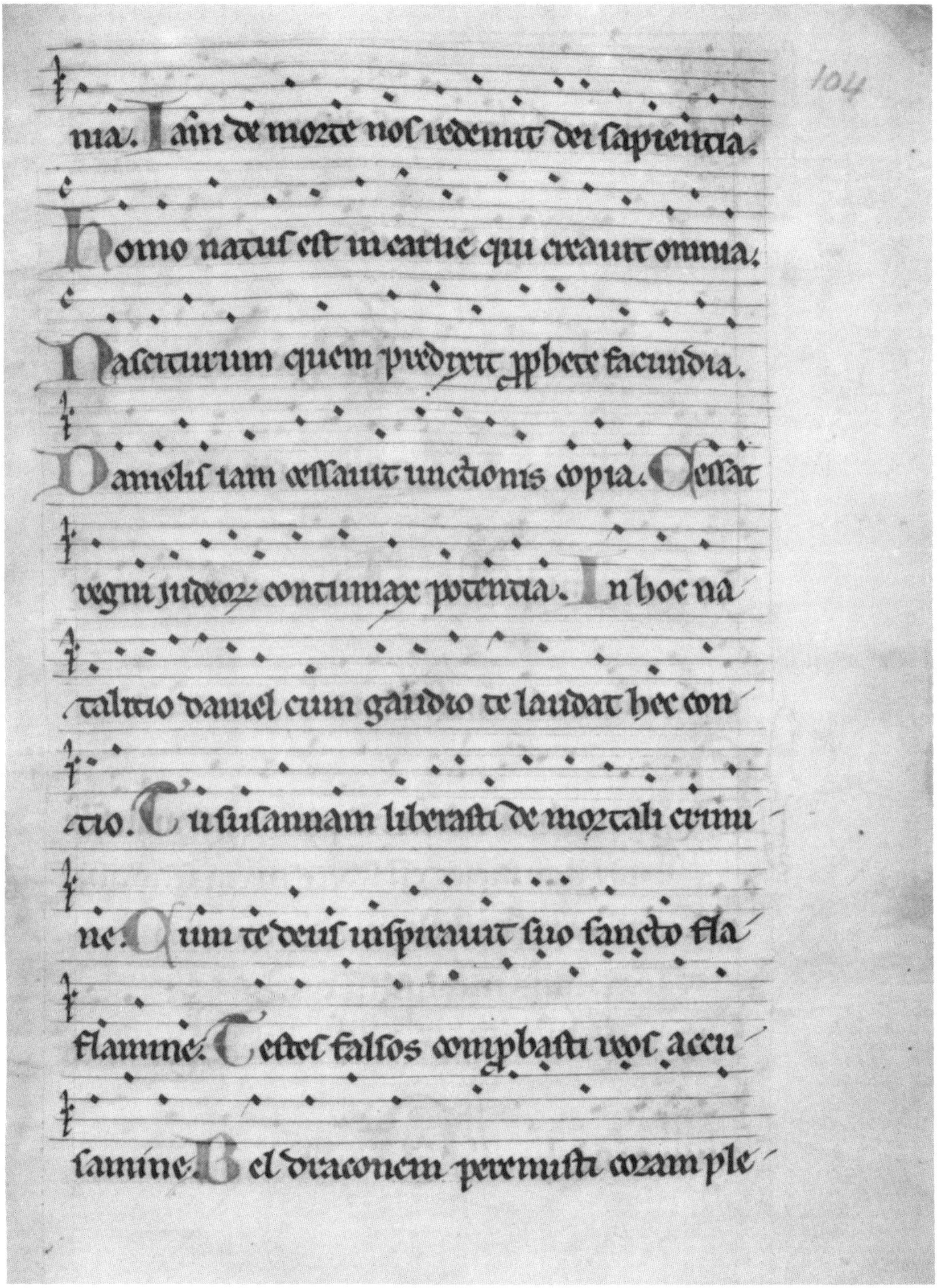

19. *Ludus Danielis*. Egerton MS. 2615, fol. 104r.

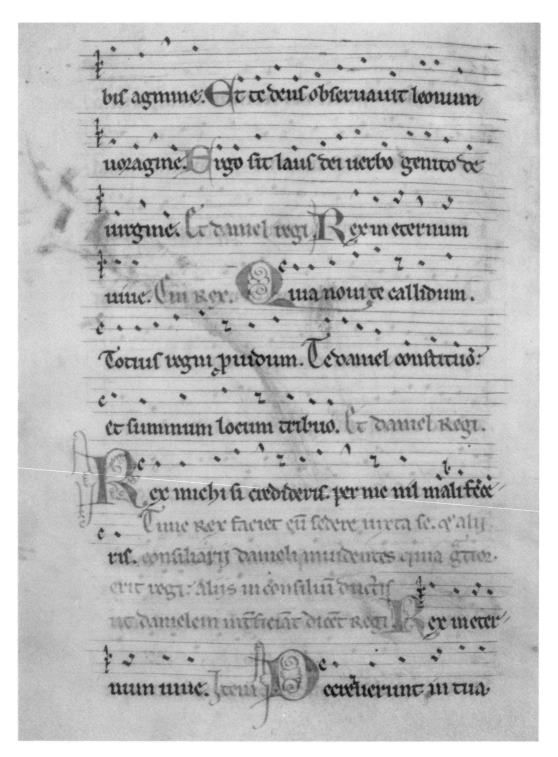

20. *Ludus Danielis*. Egerton MS. 2615, fol. 104ᵛ.

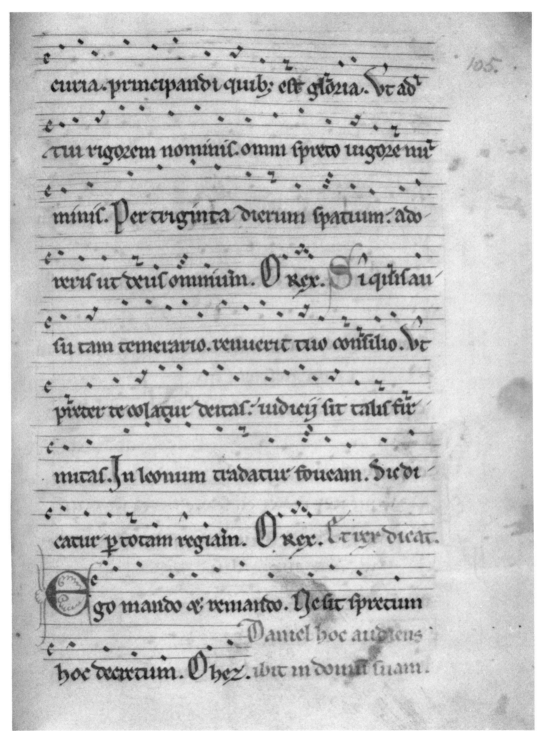

21. *Ludus Danielis*. Egerton MS. 2615, fol. 105[r].

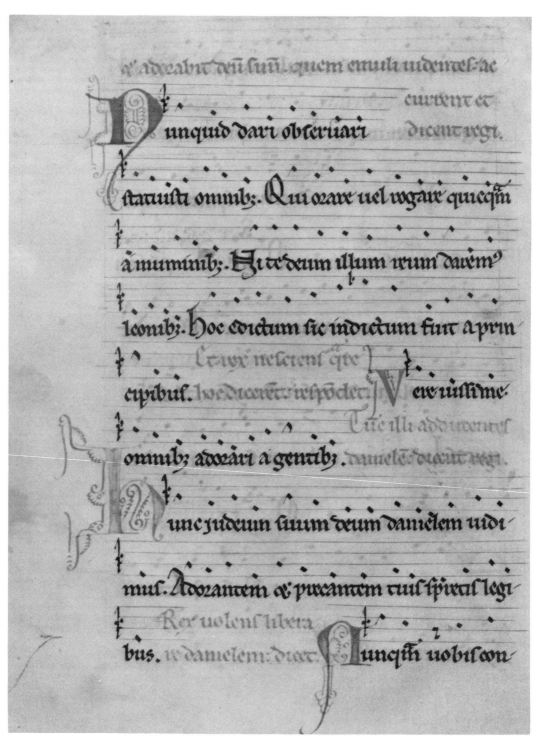

22. *Ludus Danielis*. Egerton MS. 2615, fol. 105^v.

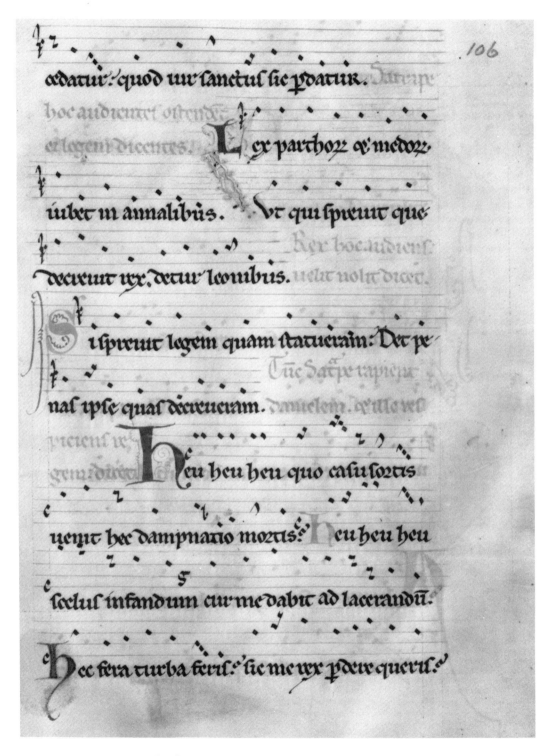

23. *Ludus Danielis*. Egerton MS. 2615, fol. 106ʳ.

24. *Ludus Danielis*. Daniel is thrown into the lions' den. Egerton MS. 2615, fol. 106ᵛ.

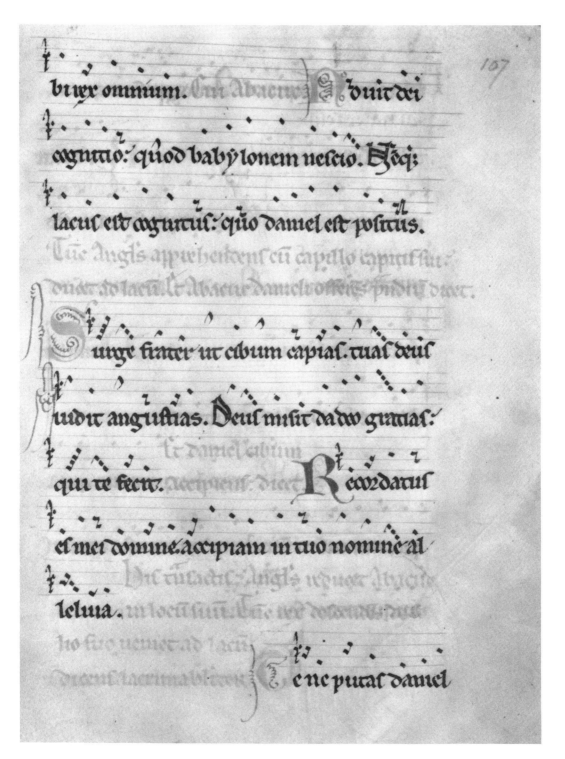

25. *Ludus Danielis.* Egerton MS. 2615, fol. 107ʳ.

salvabit ut eripiaris. Ance apposita quem

tu colis et veneraris. Rex in eter

num vive. Angelicum solita misit

pietate patronum. Quo deus ad templum con

pescunt ora leonum. Danielem

eduere: et emulos inmittere.

Merito hec patimur quia

peccauimus in sanctum dei iniuste egimus

iniquitatem fecimus. Deum danielis qui regnat

26. *Ludus Danielis.* Egerton MS. 2615, fol. 107ᵛ.

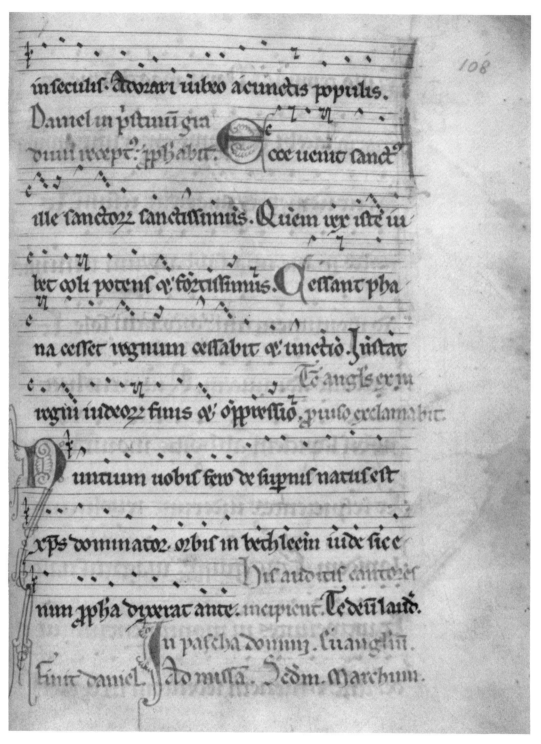

27. *Ludus Danielis*. The conclusion of the play. Egerton MS. 2615, fol. 108[r].